A CUR
E. TURNER
WORK

"When God lays hands on you, you become a Moghul."

"Many are called, few are chosen."-Matthew 22:14

DECEIVED BY BLOOD

This is not the average individual, this is a Moghul Writer®
Moghul Life presents a Moghul House Imprint®

"Deceived by Blood"

by Curtis E. Turner

DECEIVED BY BLOOD

CURTIS E. TURNER

Edited by Shanice Henry

Nation State COPYRIGHT PAGE

---

iosinom monisoi presents®
Moghul House Imprint®

For ordering please contact moghullife@gmail.com or
+1 (347) 560-9124

Soi Library of Justice
Soi Library Registration Publication Number [**SLRPN**] ™ REGISTRATION NUMBER DECEIV-C-888-04
First Soi'Ru Digital Edition 2022
Designed and Authenticated by MONI'SOI®
Under Jurisdiction of & First Released in the Soi Republic Nation/Nation State of Soi Republic®
9 8 7 6 5 4 3 2 1 0

First Printed in the Republic
First Published in the United States of America
PHILADELPHIA PENNSYLVANIA
Amexem, Al Morocco

SLRPN DECEIV-C-888-04
SOI LIBRARY OF JUSTICE® COPYRIGHT NUMBER TC-77-080-051
SOI LIBRARY CATALOGUE NUMBER 0309042028
Soi Paperback-Publication SPISBN: **66-7-386-66329-51**
Deceived by Blood® Written by Moni'soi®
SOI LIBRARY

DIGITAL DATA
Deceived by Blood E-BOOK Soi Digital International Number 0808
COPYRIGHT TC-77-080-052 SPISBN 66-7-386-66329-52
SLRPN DECEIV-C-888-05

FICTION/CRIME/

'The Brand' that is made reference to, is CURTIS E. TURNER®

Moghul Life Private Corporation {Publishing}

Ordering Information:

Quantity Sales. Special discounts are available on quantity purchases by corporations, associations, public relation & advertising agencies, and others. For details, contact the publisher at the address above.

Orders by US trade bookstores and wholesalers. Please contact Moghul Life, Publishing Department:

moghullife@gmail.com

PAPERBACK ISBN 9798370437922

Library of Congress Catalogue, LOC Number: 2022921964

Moghul House Imprint® Paperback

Deceived By Blood/Curtis Turner®/CURTIS TURNER®
The main category of the book — 1. Fiction 2. Crime 3.
Cover Designed by Artist iosinom moni'soi®

THE FIRST SOI RU' EDITION

DECEIVED BY BLOOD"

MOGHUL LIFE BOOKS®

Moghul House Imprint®
International Partner Moghul Life

USA Canada United Kingdom Australia New Zealand
Spain Africa

First Printed in the United States of America
Foreign Jurisdiction I Philadelphia, Pennsylvania
Published 2023 The Year of Jubilee-Redemption

An Imprint of Moghul Life Private Corporation ®
Authored & Written By Curtis E. Turner
Edited by Shanice Henry

DISCLAIMER:

To my wife and friend, May blessings be upon you forever more.

-C. Turner

DEDICATION

Words from Publisher,

This book is dedicated to all of those who are following hard after their dreams and vision. Curtis came to Moghul Life Private Corporation®, Publishing company eager, ready and motivated that the words that he has written are going to change lives. We don't actually know who we are attracting into our lives or why their presence is required. We do know that all living beings serve a purpose.

We dedicate this book to all of our readers and to all of his audience. We want you to know that all writers have a voice, their own style of writing. We wanted to ensure that Curtis voice as a writer would be published. We came into agreement that, 'Deceived by Blood' prospers. We are proud of you Curtis for entrusting us with this project of yours, so that as a team we shall reach the people and your literary work and film will be known at all chosen generations.

moni'soi®
Publisher

INTRODUCTION

THE PROSPERITY SOURCES WAS BORN TO BE

Deceived by Blood was born while going through a situation within my relationship. From that anger, unknowingly, I was writing a book with my vision of a movie for Tyler Perry. I put this project slash movie down for years, but it birthed from me just asking God to direct my path and lead me not to my own understanding, but to God's will for my life. I work in construction, never had a full-time job since 1990. It just wasn't in God's will in my opinion. He did however teach me the word and I have been prospering from it even in this present time. On his call, not worrying about life just living in my motto I will remain humble and blessed if I have blessed wills by His blood of continuous blessings. The years and dates of sins have destroyed the educational value of the inner brain. I sit in a world knowing the talents of God's gift are here and here I am Curtis Turner. I am here just simple with plans and a vision by his Mercy. As my journey continued the leadership lead me to a new land. I reached again for God's kind gifts and he puts angels in the hedges to guide me as I traveled 40 years in this desert. I asked for a plan to retire not from painting, but from a kingdom he built my grace. God gave me the desires of my heart to wait for myself to awake to my season. Predestined by the Almighty to take my family generations out of bondage, meaning desert. As Moses delivered by the Power of God the children of Israel but continued to be...The world and that comes to the opening of The Prosperity Sources the God has poured the talents of his child that he came Curtis Eugene Turner. Mr. Perry, I ask that in you're relating time to read, evaluate and reach out for any questions that you may have.

Thank you for your strength Father.
Curtis E. Turner

DECEIVED BY BLOOD

Story by Curtis E. Turner

My brothers and I stood around an open barrel, blazing with fire. The four of us were enjoying the night air while we warmed our hands over a bright burning fire. We laughed and joked about everything; life, love, until the million-dollar question arose that left us all contemplating.

What would you do with a million bucks?

Time passed and the night air grew colder as Gee, the youngest of us, interrupted our thoughts.

"How about a game of pool?"

With all of us in agreement we headed to the hottest Bar's in Warner Robins, Smokes Bar and Grill. After a few hours at Smokes, we went our separate ways.

As I entered my home, I got to thinking about my girl, Moncelisa, who was away for the week. She was pretty as Leonardo DaVinci's art. The Mona Lisa, and just like all relationships that have their ups and downs, our ten-year relationship was an unhappy one, but I loved her anyway. I picked up the phone to call her.

"Hello," the voice single from the other end.

Just hearing her voice made me excited, we laughed and joked for a while, then suddenly she asked to be free. Her words caught me off guard, all understanding had left me, I gripped the phone tightly before asking her to repeat herself ...

"I want my freedom," she replied.

I sat there with the phone to my ear, all kinds of thoughts racing through my mind.

"Why was she saying this to me? Is she saying we're over?"

The sound of my heart beating echoed throughout the silence of the room. There was nothing more for her to say. No explanation in the world could replace the emptiness in my gut. Feeling like a man that had just been castrated, I hung up the phone. I needed a break from my thoughts, so I took a nap.

I woke up after several hours of restless sleep. MonceLisa words dancing in my head, "Freedom, freedom,"

"God! Why does she want this?" I thought we were good.

I screamed as I covered my ears to silence the voice, it did not work. Nothing worked. The sound only grew louder. I had to do something. As I rose to my feet, a sudden dizziness came over me.

I was hurting and my mind ached with pain. How can a mind be so intelligent to create a nuclear bomb, but lack the sense to shut off hurt? I picked up the phone, not to call Moncelisa but to take some time off from work. I had a vacation coming and getting away would be the best medicine.

A week passed and I decided to visit my mother. I had to tell her about Moncelisa, but she already knew. I needed to think of a new destination to get away. Then I thought of Atlanta and just needed some space. “God may have a blessing there.”

“Why not? It's time for a change, I thought to myself. Atlanta it is! Time to resign from my job.”

I kissed my mom, told her to have a good day, that I would be in touch, and then I left for home. I started packing my things. I needed to prepare for a trip, for a new journey. I made a few calls to my family, friends, and pastor. I called my best friend Pearl and asked her to meet me to just chill for a day at Golden Corral and the park. We talked about everything just as good friends.

We were about to go our separate ways, then she hugged me tight and said, “Curtis, I will be praying for you.” I went home to get some rest. The morning came. At 4 a.m. It was time to start my new journey. The bus ride to Atlanta was a grueling one. My spirit wondered over every aspect of my life.

“Where did I go wrong? What have I done to lose the love of my life? And at what point did my life take this turn?"

Then I thought of Smokes Bar and Grill. A smile came across my face. Smokes, a place with that old bar fly appeal, where everyone was welcomed including, bikers, country folks, and even the local drug dealers. This place became the hang out spot. It was where I used to sit and chill with my brothers, playing games of pool, and tugging on the joint that would take my mind to euphoric places. I lingered over the thought. Wanting once again to smell that sweet smell of euphoria. Nevertheless, this could have been part of my downfall, not being able to concentrate on what I needed to do, by enjoying what I wanted to do.

I shook my head relinquishing the thought, then letting my mind's eye explore the many snapshots that summed up my life. I sat remembering how I attended church on a regular basis, and my many prayers to God. Only God can fix this feeling, this yearning deep inside me. Knowing I wanted to move on with my life. I had no clue on how to go about it, I went to the Lord in prayer. As the bus came to a stop, I saw that I had reached my destination, "Atlanta."

As time moved on, I knew I would need a place to stay. I grabbed a newspaper, and found a rooming house and moved in. After settling in, I made some calls. First was my Mom. She said that she spoke to Moncelisa periodically talking about how she has been trying to reach me. I thought I was beyond the stage of getting lovesick, but hearing how she was trying to reach me, it so easily angered me! It was just days ago, that she had just asked for freedom. I was not sure what was going on.

"Oh well, I thought to myself maybe it's time for me to move on and make some changes, but not as quick."

A few days had passed, and I began to look for work. Two weeks passed and still no work. Finally, I received a call for an interview as a hospital custodian. I was hired. I thanked God for the job, it was a new start. I remembered while waiting for God to put his plans together for me, so that I could begin my new life. It gave me time to work on the gifts that he had given me. I finally find time to patent my invention. In this season, still wanting to work with the Children of Israel Project, another gift that will one day be nationwide services that God wants the world to be a conquering spirit, drive. Now it's time to focus on the new city, the new job at hand. Yes, I will say, God has a plan for the Destiny of Curtis, things are really getting better.

About two months had passed since I began working at the hospital. One day, on my break, I was sitting under a tree where I was reading and meditating on Gods word when a beautiful nurse with eyes and teeth that glowed as a shadow of an angel appeared right next to me. I stared. I couldn't move my body.

She then asked, "Are you okay?"

I couldn't answer.

"Sir, Are you ok?" She asked again.

The words just came out, "I'm in love with you!"

"What?" She said.

"Oh, oh, Forgive me," I said.

She smiled with a cute little giggle.

"Really?

"Don't you think we need to be friends first?" I'm Lavonia .

Even her name was heavenly. "I'm Curtis, and the pleasure is all mine."

She went on her way, and every other day I spoke to her in the passing of the hallways.

I cleaned her nurse's station three times a day, even though it wasn't my scheduled duty, just to see her beauty. She knew that was not my station to clean. Things in the big city were getting better. I got a good job, my own apartment, a car, and new friends. The only thing was missing was a companion to help make my life sort of complete. I was not sure what was needed.

It has been a year now in the Big A, and I haven't been on a single date. Trying to focus on God and myself. I joined a good church, First United Pentecostal, after a co–worker invited me there several months ago.

One day at work my co-worker came to me and asked was I gay, right out the blue.

"Hell No" I said quickly, "Why you ask me that?"

He said, "I never see you!" Hollering at the girls.

"Oh Bro, Plenty around here! You sort of took me by surprise asking me if I'm gay!"

I replied, "It is just that I am focusing on God and his purpose for my new life."

He told me that he noticed that I get nervous around that nurse Lavonia, and suggested I ask her out? I never see her with anyone. Not even on her break.

"She's gorgeous. She probably has a man, and I may not be her type of guy. What would a beautiful woman like her possibly see in me? Then I thought why not? Hell, I am asking, Why not me?"

You'll never know until you ask." He replied.

I thought about it a minute, and said, "You know brother, you may be right, I will ask her out. But what if she's involved? Will I accept a turn down?

He said, "I don't see a ring on her finger." So, Von left for his shift and left me thinking about it until my shift ended. "Man she is gorgeous and sexy."

I walked Lavonia to the parking lot sometimes. Not to stalk her, but to simply be near her when we walked to and from the office. We would share a word with each other about the Lord and others. Nothing more than that, but today it was going to be different, I was going to ask her out. We had become friends, but I knew I was in love with her the first time I spoke to her. So, today I will build up the nerves to ask her out.

The day was long and very busy, and all I thought about was Lavonia.

Then, at that very moment my phone rang. It was my daughter calling to check on me as children always do. I talked to my grandkids, sent me a picture of my family, who I missed so very much. We talked a while, and it was a great talk. We laughed and set a time to get together, then said our goodbyes.

My break was about to be over, so I had to find Lavonia.

She walked in as I was getting up to leave the break room.

I walked over to where she was, took a deep breath, and said, “Can I ask you a question? Nervous, yes, I am."

She said, “Sure!”

Then I asked, “Are you married or involved with someone?”

“No and No.” She replied, with a smile that lit up the

room.

"Really?" I asked. "Why?" She gasped.

My self-stuttering a little, I told her I was wondering if she would like to go to dinner and a movie sometime.

She said, "Sure, why not? It's been a while."

I was overwhelmed with joy. She wrote her number in my hand, and where to meet her as well. I thought to myself, my hand has been touched by an angel, I may never wash it again. We set a date.

"Call me. I may already be there." She stated.

Then she went on with her day. The date was set for Friday night, and it was already Thursday afternoon. I was smiling and dancing with the broom all day. Von walked up, and asked what all the dancing was about? I grabbed him by the shoulders and shook him.

She said, "YES!"

I replied, "We're going on a date," I told him.

"We who?" He asked.

"Lavonia and me." She said, "Yes!" I informed him.

"Well, that's great bro, make your first impression a good one." Then we went back to work.

The day seemed longer than usual, but it gave me hours to think about tomorrow's date. What to wear? What to say? How to win? Finally, the day ended, and off I went to the barber shop. After, I shopped, grabbed a bite, and left for home.

I felt like a kid preparing for the first day of school. I laid my clothes out and was in bed by 9pm. Then the phone range, and to my surprise, it was Moncelisa. She told me I was wrong for leaving her, and that I didn't come after her, again I though she moved on.

"What?" Loudly I replied.

I've spent 10 years chasing you.

Then she said, "I love you, but you will pay for this."

This time she knew it was over, no chasing. In her voice it was anger, bitterness, deceit, and revenge, but why? I had moved on, now she wanted back in. This was our dream from the start to move to Atlanta, start a life. I told Moncelisa goodbye.

She was still talking when I hung up. She was really heated. I turned my phone off. Nothing was going to interfere with Friday. At 8:45 I hit the sheets.

The next morning, my mother called just to see how I was doing. She asked if I was coming home for the family reunion on the Fourth of July.

"Yes, mother," I replied. "Little did she know, a celebration was taking place."

We chatted for a while, and off I went to work. This is the day I get to be with the most beautiful woman in Atlanta.

Smiles all day while getting my supplies together, brother Von approached asking when the big day is, I smiled even harder and told him, "Today!" Bro. Today.

He said, "Oh, that's why you are singing, huh?"

"Yep, you bet." I said, still smiling, "Good luck, and hit me up afterwards."

Its break time. I was scared in a way to see Lavonia, but she's sitting at the spot looking around, as if she was looking for me to show up.

"Hi, Curtis! Listen, I have something to say."

Now I'm worried that she's going to cancel the date, my first date, but if so, it's a good reason.

Then she goes on. "I haven't been on a date in a few years. So, I want you to know that I'm a little rusty. Haven't been with a man in sometime."

"Why is she testing me? Now I'm thinking fresh with spider webs, a man thing. I'm smiling as if this was an invitation to intimacy. Please don't be late okay."

She said. I'm prompt for this night. It's 3:30, time to clock out. I ran into her in the parking lot. She smiles and waved good bye gently. So, I go to Von's house to hang out for a minute, and then it's 5pm and time to head home. To prepared myself to get all GQ; I get dressed and I'm out the door to my destination, putting the address in my GPS. I arrived, parked, and walked up to the building taking a big deep breath before walking in.

She was waiting by the door, wearing a pearly white evening gown and her hair down, not pinned up as usual. Never seen it like that, fresh nails, little jewelry. Looking as God's gift to not just men, but for me. I'm standing there with my mouth open.

Again, she asked, "Are you okay?"

"Yes, I am. You are a beautiful woman," I said. Now I'm thinking, Why she don't have a man? Wow. We enter the building, I'm not aware of the sign on the door. 1st United Church of Pentecostal.

"Yes! We're at church."

The exciting part was we both are Pentecostal. We enjoyed the message which was "God has a gift for you. Believe it or not, I want this woman." As any gift.

After service we went to Bay Breeze Seafood. I left my car at church. We both liked seafood. We laughed because we realized that we had many things in common. So, we continued to chill and talk about God, not realizing it was now 11pm.

I asked, "Are you ready to leave?"

"Not really," she said. "There's some place I'd like to take you. We'll take your car home." She said.

We left the restaurant and went back to the church parking lot to get my car. She followed me to my place, so I rode with her. We ended up at a park, where there were still many people out at twelve midnight and flowers blooming, like a garden patch in heaven. "It's a fine night."

She blended in with the sight. "This is where I come for peace and inventory of myself," She said. "It's beautiful with the proper lighting, and she fitted in."

"Oh yeah! I know it was too quick, but I grabbed her hand as we walked along the walkway, exploring waterfalls, ducks, and springs. Two lonely people on a date, she looked me in my eyes."

“What took you so long to ask me out?” She asked.

Now I’m speechless! I stuttered a second. “I didn’t see where you’d be interested in a mop boy.”

She giggled. “I noticed how much you read the word and I didn’t see a ring on your finger. I wanted to ask you, but I couldn’t pull myself to ask a man out to a movie.”

I thought man! She noticed me all this time, but they say good things come to those that wait, and I’m overdue. As we were leaving, she asked was there any woman in my life? “No,” I said. “It’s been 16 months.”

“You’ve been counting huh?” She giggled.

“YES!”

I replied “Like clockwork.”

We ended the night in a suburb community, pulling up in a yard, the garage door opens and she parks. Now I’m thinking how this date going to end.

We entered into a warm beautiful home. “Make yourself at home,” She said.

"There's cheese and crackers on the stand, and wine in the fridge."

Now it's 2:15 a.m. and all kinds of thoughts going on in my head. But hey, we're adults. I took my shoes off, suit coat, and tie, and did as she asked, made myself at home. Mellow jazz playing from somewhere, then she appears with a negligee on with silk pants of course, hair pinned up, she brought a blanket out of the closet, asking did I mind staying the night.

There goes the stuttering again, "For sure!" I said.

"You can sleep here, the remote is there. Good night. She said."

She hugged me, and I kissed her on the forehead, and she went upstairs. You already know I'm thinking booty call or she's really trusting me on the first date? I turned the TV on watched a movie and fell asleep.

It's morning and I'm awakened by an amazing smell of breakfast being set up in front of me with a greeting smile.

"I'll take you home after breakfast, and if you like we can spend the day together." She stated.

She was reaching for what she wanted. Me. I was all down with all her needs.

Now my thinking changed, wondering, "Is she mental, disturbed, controlling, Or just in the need of a friend?

I've had my share of nut cases. And you just don't know. I'm checking medicine cabinets, glove boxes purses. So, we left for medication and arrived too my place. She sat on the couch, as if we've known each other a long time. Nice place you have Curtis, who is your decorator. She wasn't wasting any time to get this man, as weeks passed to months of dating, no intimacy but we do sleep under one another. I tried to make a move on her on the couch. The 4th of July is coming up, going to invite her to meet my family.

My daughters and nine grands, and of course my sons, whether we get along or not, will be good to see them all together this weekend.

"Do you have anything planned for the weekend?" I asked Lavonia if she would accompany me to my hometown, and she said yes.

"What do you have in mind? I'm down."

I said I'll pick you up at 8a.m, dress casual and bring something to change into, if we go out. Lavonia and I went to visit our friend Von. Von, who's my best friend and like a brother to me. His girlfriend just made it back to town, after a two week visit with her family. They are our new best friends. So, we headed out picked up some wine and other things. We got there and they were hanging out at the gazebo like always.

Von and I walked off while the women chatted. Von just came out and said, “That’s it! That’s it! I need you to ride somewhere with me.”

Not telling me anything at all, we ended up at the jewelry store.

“I love her C. I’m going to ask her to marry me!” He said.

I’m thinking go for it, I feel they really loved each other enough to be married. I asked Von, “Have you ever discussed marriage with Glo?”

“Nope but today, I am,” He said excitedly.

“What are you going to feel like if she says no?” I asked.

“Then, we’ll work up to a yes.”

I brought his desire down a little but didn't destroy it.

“I’m going to ask her Curtis.”

This a name he never used, unless he was determined or scared. “I love her bro!”

I told him that I wished all the luck with this. "Now, let's pick out a ring," I said.

He shopped, and my phone rang. It was Lavonia , saying pick up some horse shoes, and to think we were right next door to a western shop. It had spurs, hats, and the most important thing, horse shoes. By the time I made my purchase, Von came out the jewelry store and showed me the ring he picked.

I said, "Man that'll get her finger cut off." He giggled Thinking is this his life savings he just spent on this ring?

"Wow, man that's some ring!" I admired.

"Let's ride C."

My heart thumping to find out this blessing. When we arrived, the girls were still under the gazebo. The girls were preparing for the evening.

Finally, Von said, "I feel good about this Curtis! I really do."

The girls walked up giggling looking at Von like, oh you been bad. We joined hands in prayer, then Von said, "Hello friends and Glo. I have a very important and beautiful thing I'd like to ask Glo. Will you marry me?"

Right out the blue, she turned around to him. He's right in front of her kneeling down to complete the proposal, and she says nothing. She didn't say a word. She just stared down at him. Von there is something I need to tell you.

She's looking scared, but then it changed. "I'm with child!"

We all gasped. "Are you mad?" She asked. "Say something Von."

"Glo this is the will of God I'm asking you to marry me, we're with child, this is a gift," Von said.

"Yes, I will marry you!" Glo said excitedly.

We all gathered and prayed together again. This one day, Von wanted something, and I've always admired him for his faith. Lavonia and I decided to leave and let the happy couple enjoy this moment, planning for the rest of their lives. Von did say it was a good day. I just knew then he had a revelation. Lavonia had tears in her eyes. She said it was so romantic with the presence of God. She said Glo better pick me for the maid of honor.

That's my girl, I thought. I dried her tears as we went to the other side of the house to chill. This was our chill spot. Von doesn't have to be home, we can just go there.

"A warm garden, Let's not talk about them let's talk about us."

I only have two questions for you, "Do you trust God? Do you trust me?"

She said yes to both.

"Then will you marry me?"

"Are you serious Curtis?" With the biggest smile on her face.

"Damn right I am."

"Yes, I will." She answered excitedly.

Now this was a real good day. The moment of their joy thrilled my inner love for Lavonia and me. I knew she had replaced every bandage on my once broken heart, and filled it with a new-found love, so much different from my other relationships. It was on and off like a revolving door.

This seemed real, and it was! We sat and talked and rejoiced in our new beginning. Discussing when we were going to let them know. We'll invite them out to dinner and spring it on them, meanwhile, we will work on the date. I took her home to get ready for our trip down south to meet her future family. I called mother to tell her the good news about my engagement. I asked her not to say a word about it and that I was bringing Lavonia home for the 4th of July.

She seemed so happy for me, that I had moved on. She said Moncelisa was not too happy about the last time we talked, when I hung up on her. Pissed is the word that I got.

It really filled my heart with joy that she was now on the hurting end. It also showed me that in spite of everything she still cared for me. From that last conversation that would've gotten crazy if I didn't hang up
but to say silently, I still cared for her too, but that has passed. Now, with a new life ahead of me and the past forever gone, Lavonia and I grew stronger.

We started praying together on God's gifts of abundance. She meant a lot to me. God has given me a woman, a nurse, my nurse for the aches and pains. To heal me without measures.

We were at my place on a Saturday. Von and Glo stopped by to ask about being a maid of honor, the best man for Lavonia, and I to take part in their wedding. The girls talked colors, place, and other things for the wedding.

Von and I walked out by the garden. He looked at me with a tear in his eye and said, "Bro I'm happy! God is good."

I replied all the time and that I was happy for him. I said, "Glo loves you, and you are about to be a husband and father."

We walked back to the screened porch. Lavonia looked at me giving me a signal with her head, I guess it is time to let them know, I said guys we have something to share.

Lavonia burst out, "We're getting married!" And now all joy comes from us all.

No questions, when did this happen?

"That's great!"

Von and I decided to go out and get a celebratory wine and cracker basket, mixed with a little this and a little that. We talked about everything. The wedding, the baby, and then Von said, "Hey C how about a double wedding?"

I'm saying why not, "Lets spring it on the girls when we get back."

Traffic was backed up, a wreck on 285. We called to inform the girls. Finally reached my place, we rushed in to discuss this wedding, but before we could sit down good, the girls say, we want a double wedding. Von and I just looked at each other and said, “Why not?” -With laughter.

We just knew God was listening. The night was getting to be over. Von, Glo, and Lavonia decided to leave because we had to get an early start to Warner Robins. We kissed and said our goodbyes. I’m sitting, just thinking of the love of my life, who has been my friend, then my girl, and now going to become my wife.

I deserved this .... As much hell I’ve been through, I prepared for the night, the phone rang Lavonia and I always called each other when we got home, we talked for
a while about the plans for tomorrow; little did she know I’m taking her to meet my family. First mom, then the children and grands. We said our good nights, "I’ll pick you up at 7a.m.”

And to bed I went. The morning came. I picked
Lavonia up and we hit 75 south.

An hour and 45 minutes later and we were pulling up at my mother’s house. I called from the car, to see was she awake and she was. I’m at the front door, Lavonia and I got out the car, sat on the front porch. I knew mother would be a while, she's 78 and I left my keys. Finally, she opened the door.

I hugged her, "How have you been my shorty?"

That's what I call her because she is four foot tall.

"Lavonia this is my mother, and mother this is my bride to be."

I saw my cousins Franklin and Anna, who lives across the street, I noticed them standing out, so I yelled, "What's up cuz?"

I walked away, mother and Lavonia sat and talked. I saw the look Lavonia was giving me like (don't leave me here) but I kept walking, chatted with my folks, asked them to come meet the next Mrs. Turner. And we walked across mother's yard. I introduced them, and Franklin and I talked about the Fourth of July plans. I asked my mother to get dressed because I wanted her to spend the day with us, it was early.

My niece Erika and Tay were not at home at the time. Lavonia helped mother while my cousin and his wife sat out under the car port talking more about the 4th of July plans, the set up. The only thing missing was a place and the invitations has not been sent out. We only have two weeks' time to find the right location, mother and Lavonia came outside, and my mother said, "I like her already."

Mother didn't like to ask for help, like I said Lavonia was different, that made her soul complete. We said our goodbyes, loaded up, and I took my mother to Forsyth, Georgia to Shoney's; a place she once worked in Warner Robins. After she stopped working, we always ate there, until they closed Shoney's.

"Shoney's," she was said excited like a child, at the ice cream truck. I haven't seen a Shoney's in 30 years. We entered to be seated, menu in hand, whatever you want mother. For a little woman she ate a lot, a lot of good foods of course. We sat a little and talked.

"When is the big day," my mother asked?

"We haven't set a date yet." I replied.

"I do wish you both well. I love you, Curtis." Thank you, we paid the check and left. On the way home, we stopped in Macon to see my daughter Nicki and her family. Luckily everyone was home, her husband and her 5 children. Boy were they happy to see us. Been some time, I introduced them all to Lavonia. They hit it off right away.

It was 10:30 in the morning. We stayed an hour then left and ended up at my mother's church. She wasn't aware this was part of the day, and I didn't want her to miss church. A great sermon titled, "Family need to come together, after the one o clock service."

I called Amethyst, my oldest daughter, married mother of three to see if they were home and they were. I told her to expect me within the hour, and we headed to Perry, Georgia. We arrived at her house; the girls greeted us. They have grown so much, and the girls liked Lavonia. It was just something about her people liked. We enjoyed the time we spent. Left for my mother's house I didn't want to visit anymore relatives today. We stayed at my mothers till 5 p.m. then headed back to Atlanta. We talked and I threw the idea out about her family joining us for the 4th. She said she would call them later on today. We've only met once, and it was brief. Once we reached Atlanta we went by our place where we liked to eat. On the way Lavonia just came out with it.

"Let's get married next week," she said with joy, I almost ran off the road.

"What?" So exciting like a child getting a new toy.

I pulled over at a store, parked, and yes, she said we can put in a leave of absence, and elope to Vegas. I'm thinking let's do it! We laughed now I'm thinking about expenses. Don't worry about the cost, my father loves me, and he'll be happy that we were married. Even though my parents know we are not intimate.

"What?" I asked with a lot of expressions.

"Yes, my father is Bishop Dupree."

"You mean the minister I've seen on Sunday, and Tuesday on TV?"

"Yes, one in the same," she replied. "Now are you really sure?" I asked.

She said yes, and no one must know until the 4th celebration. Let's do it, we will still meet with Von and Glo to explain and to help them plan a nice and beautiful wedding. So, home we went to discuss where we'd live. Her place of course is where she decided. I let the landlord know and it was no problem.

We left and went to her place, took out a pen and pad we made notes together. What she wanted out of the house, the garage, to set a date for a yard sale. She said we would buy all new furniture. She had it all planned out to a T, My kind of woman.

First, we set a date for both, yard sales to take place, the same two days. We went to get signs and put them up. The day was about to be over. Monday is coming, going to put in some leave time.

The day came with rain, got to work. Von met me at the door, "What's up little brother?"

Something he sometimes calls me. "Tomorrow at 3 o'clock right?"

"Yep! Glad when all this is over with. I got Las Vegas on my mind."

Von and I didn't see each other as much, because my job changed from Custodian to Supervisor Engineer, where I wrote schedules, and supply lists for over nine employees. God showed his favor within a year. The thing is Von is now one of my employees and he wasn't pissed.

We're brothers by God and he was more of second in command.

Lavonia texted me to meet her under the tree for lunch. I couldn't wait to see her. Now it's the middle of the week. I finally got a response for my leave which is Friday to Friday, and today was Wednesday. Lunch came about, she had her leave papers in hand smiling with a little song.

"We're going to Vegas, and we're going to get married everything is ready. Going to have the yard sales next Thursday, get married Saturday, then back to work by the following Monday.

Saturday came around, two places with yard sales, she's home and I'm at my place, the yard sale stopped at 7 pm. I've sold $310.00 worth of unneeded stuff and about $100 more to go.

I left to go to Lavonia 's, I stopped by the bank, deposited $250 and flashed her way.

Her yard sale was still going on. So, I attended as a customer. I noticed a man constantly observing a vase that had $10 on it. Finally, I picked up that same vase, he was watching me, I walked up to Lavonia and said, "Miss how much is this vase?"

"She's with me, $10 it's late," she said. The gentleman walked up, I saw $20 on it, yes but it's late.

"I'll give you $15," I said.

"$20 the gentleman said this beautiful vase is at least worth $100."

I guess he know prices of crystal even when it's used. He said, "Ma'am I'll give you $50 and forget the bidding"

"Sold, too rich for my blood."

She smiled as I walked away. Wrapped the vase and he left. She just shook her head. A love seat $35, I told this customer this is nice, the lady said $35 that's a steal. Miss is $35 the actual price for this $25 since its late $30, $35 here we go again?

Lavonia just giggling as she had to walk away, $40. Ma'am I'll give you $50, for this love seat and lamp that matched $75. Well, again too rich for my blood, she sold it. Ma'am if you don't mind, I'll help you load it up and I did.

Lavonia said baby with a smile you should have been a salesman, then I said, "Yeah right! No more customers tomorrow will be for the yard sale."

Lavonia talked about how she made $600. Must have from what I saw. Very expensive items, we sat and laughed about the bidding, and then she said excuse me, and went in the house, then came back with two glasses of iced tea.

"Curtis in an hour I want to take you somewhere," she said with a smile.

"Okay."

The hour approached and we left. Stopped at Papa Johns and she says she will be right back. She returned with a buggy full of pizzas. I helped her load them in her SUV.

“What’s up babe?” I asked.

"Just be patient honey,” she said.

We drove for about an hour to Conyers, Georgia, pulling up to a building. It was dark and when we entered, about 15-20 kids ran up to Lavonia like a kid that’s happy to see their parent. They rushed her to the floor, I never seen her laugh as much. The kids loved her. “Baby these are my children in which I help take care of,” she said.

“Wow I didn’t know," I said.

Community development is a calling for God’s gift to open someday and my bride to be knows this and at that moment I knew she was heaven sent and that this relationship was in line with God. We stayed until 11:30; she’s great with the kids. Reading stories, while they stuffed their faces with pizza, a few fell asleep. We said our goodbyes and we headed back home.

I drove because I knew she was tired. On the road I talked about how good she was with the kids, not knowing I was talking to myself; she was sound of sleep. Finally, we made it to her place. I reclined her seat and covered her with my jacket. I didn't want to wake her, so I did the same, we slept in the car.

At 6am she woke up saying, "Curtis why didn't you wake me?"

"You were tired I didn't see a reason to," I replied then we went inside.

She showered, while I cooked breakfast. We ate and started preparing for the final day of the yard sale. I left went home and took a shower, opened the garage door to set up my tables to pray for this day. Cars driving up at 7:30 a.m. I didn't have much more to sell, just going to let everything go for one price.

Listen up, there's over $200 worth of merchandise, I'm letting all go for $150! Two customers looking around, one said I'll take it, and the other said $160. I wasn't trying to start a bidding war, but I ended up getting $185. I helped box up the stuff and loaded it for them, took the sign down, went inside, and went back to sleep. When I got up it was after three in the afternoon.

Lavonia had called several times, didn't bother checking my messages. I called her back. She answered.

"Are you okay?"

"Yes," I said.

"I got worried since I didn't hear from you," she said.

"I'm good how did your sale go," I asked?

"I sold most of its bout a $160 more left to sell. Goodwill will be picking up the rest," she said.

I let her know that I would pick her up in about an hour. I took a shower again and I didn't dress casually, but tonight its special. I found time to buy the ring in which it didn't matter to her. I locked the house down and headed to my girl's place. I arrived just when she entered my car.

She kissed me gently with a smirk on her face. "Where to?"

"Just somewhere to getaway for the moment," I replied.

We drove for a couple of hours. When we arrived at our destination, she was asleep. She had no clue about what was about to take place. But I'm excited for her. I parked the car and blindfold my lady for about three minutes.

While I was blindfolding her, she asked "What are you doing Curtis?"

"I'm loving my woman, nothing more."

"You are up to something again," she replied.

She allowed me to blindfold her even though she didn't like it. We exit the car and walk about one hundred fifty feet. We entered a place like a building. Walking into a small room and exiting like on to the balcony. Finally, the movement set forth to a journey out. She took off the blindfold slowly and open her eyes.

She gasps for air holding her breathe. "Oh my God. Oh my God. A cruise ship," she said excitedly!

I told her this was no cruise. It's a four-hour tour ferry boat ride around the river of Savannah Georgia. Yes, we were finally getting away for a while. Something that we enjoyed. GETTING AWAY!

We enjoyed each other's company all day. The ferry had three levels. A dance floor level. A food level, A casino level.

After our four-hour getaway we strolled the Riverfront of Savannah and headed back home. We grabbed a meal and went to her place took a shower but this time together!

We washed each other bodies. This was the first time

I've been this close to this beautiful coke bottle, soft gentle, body! Oh, I said that. Body preserved just for me, what's about to happen maybe? Maybe this is the night, to make love to her. And float the night away.

We ended up on the bear skin rug with pillows, with candles burning and a soft jazz cd playing. We drunk some wine, laid there in each other's comfort, and then I felt that I just can't take this passionate woman anymore! I'm going to make my move to see how far it goes. Its warms me when we are kissing, one thing leads to another. The most incredible lovers who want to love, fantasy happened, yes happened.

We fell asleep, finally after 3pm we slept under each other as if we were Siamese twins again. It was a lovely moment as we laid in each other's arms. Its three hours before time for work. Only four days and we're out of here! Off to Las Vegas. The morning arose, alarm going off, took another shower together, ate a lite breakfast and off to work we went. Today as we crossed paths we looked into each other's eyes and myself, I melted.

A break was coming up for lunch, maybe just for kicks. I text baby to meet me at my place, I'll be scared to death if she said OKAY, but it was just a thought, she's so beautiful I can't wait till this workday end. Set the mood at my place to just go for it again, but don't flatter my son head. I waited on a message to return.

I got no response but when I got home her car was parked in the driveway. I walked into musical notes of Keith Sweat playing and what I had in mind, it was already prepared and in play, it happened again, and it was her call, she laid in my arms.

She asked what took you so long to get home. We drifted into the day and slept. A knock at the door woke us, it was Von and Glo.

"We got our date, July 10th."

We promised to be there for them. They asked had we got our date yet. "No," I replied.

We just didn't want them to know it was this weekend. We hung out for a while, "Everything is ordered cake included," she said. "Complete the planning we only had 14 days left from now."

Von and Glo decided to leave, and now it's another evening gone.

We stayed in and watched TV, trying to rest the day away. To be on the route to commitment, responsibility, but to be a husband, but I can't. I must take it one day at a time. I wonder was Lavonia staying the night or going home. I'm going to draw her a bath, put her favorite powder on the sheets and watch her sleep, I did just that. I never ran her a bath before. She said I was spoiling her. I told her that she deserves it and more.

I asked God to allow me to help take care of you by any means necessary. She smiled as she got in the tub filled with bubbles, I felt some type of way as I watched her beautiful body, dark and lovely is what I called her! I left the bathroom and went to the den, called a friend Ed from Warner Robins just to see what's up with things down that way.

We talked about the business he started; he said things were going well. I told him my good news, he joked

Moncelisa is going to kill you man, he laughed so did I. He knew how things with us use to be. Bro that has been over with for some time now I said, the reception will be when we get back on the 4th. No location yet but I will call you, please bring your friend.

He said congratulations and yeah make sure you call me, we hung up. Lavonia came and laid on the sofa putting her head in my lap. I saw her brush on the stand, I begin to stroke her hair and next thing I knew she was asleep. And this time with a little snore, she's tired. I eased her head onto a pillow and covered her up. When the alarm went off, I noticed her cuddled up under me. I got up to prep for work and so did she. I got in the shower, and she joined me. I was wondering if I was about to get my bones jumped before work again, but no it was innocent. No bones jumping for Curtis this morning. We got dressed and off to work we went.

Wanting to talk to Von about the duties in which he must take responsibility for while I'm gone on vacation, as little did, he know I will be married when I return, and will Announce this at the 4th of July celebration. Von was in the parking lot when we pulled up. Lavonia spoke and went to her office, "See you after work and make sure you don't forget about the 4th of July celebration."

I left to call my cousin Little Franklin to see if they found a place yet, yeah because he said, the Fountain Park, now I can call the ones I invited, and the invitation should be out on Facebook. This is going to be a grand day! I went to my office to check my schedule and assignments, there's a memo in my mailbox, from the main office asking that I call Mr. Dorsey that's my boss. I called, his receptionist answered, gave her my message.

"Yes Mr. Turner I am to inform you that there will be a mandatory meeting today at 3 p.m.," she said.

"Thank you," I said.

It's 2 o'clock now, Lavonia called to ask where we were going to dinner later.

She said, "I'm going to go with Glo to help pick out her wedding colors."

I guess that's my cue to get with Von on his tuxes. I got a text from my mom to call her ASAP, at least I thought it was her cause it came from her phone. I kept calling leaving messages, but no response and my mind was racing.

I called my sister and my niece no response. Now I'm thinking something's wrong and I should drive down there, but I will just wait a while. Finally, the phone rang, it was my niece saying my sister Deborah had a stroke and was in the hospital, but doing okay. I got a little disturbed because I couldn't reach anyone.

"I will take a minute and pray, call me if anything changes. I love you."

Now it's time for my meeting, it lasted for about an hour, it came down to promotions and moving on.

I received a new job at another hospital as head of Maintenance Engineering in Marietta, Georgia. This means I must give someone else my job, and I knew who's good at it, my man Von! This will not take place for several weeks with all that's going on, I'll just wait until after another month when everything's finalized. One more day my girl and I will be on our way to Las Vegas, never been to this place but Lavonia has several times, the day is just about over, went by fast. Two more hours and we're going shopping for the tux and whatever else my bro needed, we discussed the wedding date. Then the phone rang it was Moncelisa.

"Hello Xtian," that's the name we shared for years.

"Hello Moncelisa," I said.

We talked without bitterness; it was a pleasant conversation. Now I'm thinking she's up to something.

Maybe mother told her about my engagement, on in the conversation she began to cry I wanted to ask WHY? I really did, but this would just prolong the conversation and

I had things to do. I did ask how the family was, she said their fine, good I replied. Mona, I must go I'm at work, she asked will I be coming home soon, I'd really like to see you.

"I will be in Warner Robins soon. I would like to discuss matters with you."

I informed her, "Please go on with your life."

I felt her tears more strongly in pain as she said, "I will see you soon," then the phone went dead.

All at the same time I'm thinking why I did that. Not going to stress it. Von came by my office asking what my plans after work was.

I told him, "Hey bro whatever you need I'm down. I'll meet you at Elliot's Formal wear on Peachtree around 4:00!"

"See you there," he said. I set back thinking about Moncelisa, this life was ours. But not to dwell on it, at that time the love of my life walked through he door.

"Hey boo," she said with a smile, but she saw my thoughts were distant.

"You okay," she asked? "Not getting cold feet, are you?"

"Oh no, Moncelisa just called, she was crying, we had

a peaceful conversation for a change," I said.

"Really?" She replied.

"Hum I don't trust her with a 50-foot pole."

"Anyway boo, Glo and I are going out after work to find her colors and other stuff for the wedding. I'll call you once I get home."

We kissed and she went on. A woman's intuition to never trust another woman. Time winding down, its clock out time! Won't see this office for a week. So, I left to go meet with Von, and when I pulled up, I saw Von sitting outside of Elliott's Boutique. I walked up to him and the first thing out his mouth was.

"Bro, I'm ready to get this over with, I mean I'm going to be a husband and father. After the 4th of July celebration I'm going to talk to Glo about it."

"Hey bro, do it you'll be much happier. Have you and your girl set you date yet?"

I said, "No!" But little did he know it was this weekend.

"Make it soon C, we don't live forever that's for sure!"

We walked into the tuxedo shopped looked around at the different styles, then he called Glo to see if she has chosen a color, but she hasn't at this point.

Now, he feels a little upset. "Calm down, bro! I think its best that the two of you get together and do this."

"Absolutely, little bro. I'm sorry I wasted your time."

"Hey. We are in this together. Let's go to our spot, shoot some pool, and kick it for the rest of this evening." And that's what we did, a bar and grill called, Smooth.

We were sitting at the bar watching the news. The bartender brought two drinks over, same as we were drinking. We didn't order another. The two ladies at the booth sent them and asked if we could join them. We looked.

"Hey, why not?"

Von asked, not thinking of our girls...

"What harm can it do? Just chilling."

We walked over to the table. "You guys must be brothers, because you favor one another."

Lame pickup line.

I responded, "Yes, we are brothers in Christ. But to think we're in a bar getting gassed."

"Just enjoying life on life's own terms." It was a night out, not thinking of the time. We came here at 5:00pm. It's 11:00 pm now. My, how time flies!

We shot pool with the ladies, had salsa and chips. Then I felt it was time to go. Like a bachelor party I didn't tell my baby about. I looked at Von.

"Let's get out of here."

The ladies gave us a phone number and said, "Call us. We enjoyed you 'Brothers in Christ."

They giggled, and we went on our way, too buzzed to drive. So, instead of driving, we called a cab. But we're going to have to get up early. Von must be at work and Lavonia, and I are leaving around 10:00am. She wanted to visit her parents to break the news. And I'll get the chance to meet them again. I do hope that they will give us their blessing. Her father likes me whether he's a minister or not.

Her mother says all the time, "You enjoy life only once. Keep it in the blessing of the Lord." That's the way her mother spoke.

Von and I arrived at my place. He called Glo. I called my Boo.

She answered. "Where the hell have you been? I've been trying to reach you for hours!"

This side, I had never encountered. She was worried and hysterical. I explained, “Time just went by, Now, I'm wondering if I should tell her about the ladies."

“Hell, no!”

I apologized for not calling. We spoke for a while. I asked her could she pick me up early to go get my car.

“Yes,” she said not asking where it is.

We said goodnight. I laid down my head, spinning like a top. But I did fall asleep, finally.

The clock went off, like every morning, at 6:00am. I kicked it to the floor. I need more sleep, but I couldn't get back to sleep. I'm wondering if I should tell her about the ladies. I called Von because I knew he was up and out to get his car for work. I asked Von what he told Glo.

He said, “She didn't ask.” I said we were just doing the man things.

I'm saying, “Good. Hey, little brother, I'll call you later. Hit me up. Okay, Von?” And then I fell back to sleep. Two hours later I awaken to the smell of breakfast breezing by my nose. Grits, eggs and pancakes. Man! She has spoiled me.

"Wake up, hon. Got to get started. Long day. I want to apologize about snapping, but I was worried. Neither Glo nor myself couldn't reach you guys."

She had this look. An untrusting Curtis looks. Never heard her innocence curse before. Never seen her nervous. Something was troubling her. Now, I'm losing the taste for this breakfast. But I ate anyway. I just came out with it.

"Baby, what's wrong? Are you getting cold feet?"

"No silly," she said.

"I felt alone when I couldn't reach you. It's like my world was empty."

"Baby, I'm here until death do us part." She looked at me.

"Please don't ever leave me."

She had this look that I've never seen. A look of fear. Now, I'm wondering, "Do she has a mental problem?"

Her eyes stretched as she gazed into mine. The reason I said this, "I've been around a lot of mentally disturbed people. But today, I've never seen this side of her. And again, I apologized. But still, my mind is wondering about that look that could kill. But it's too late to call the wedding off, do pray all is good."

Tomorrow, we leave for Las Vegas. Saturday is the day we get married and enjoy the rest of our lives together. The day is no older. Going to go home to pack and wait on the moving company to get the rest of the furniture for delivery to my new home at Lavonia 's.

The phone rang. It was my baby saying she needs to talk with me later today. The truck arrived. There was a knock at the door. I open the door. The moving company came in and took care of everything. Then they followed me to Lavonia's so that I can put the furniture where needed.

I called my Boo. She asked to meet her at the Varsity for dinner. When I reached her, she said to please take a seat and she started talking without a hug, even.

"Curtis, I'm sorry about earlier. I know we never talked about my past. But I have been screwed over a couple of times and I was engaged. I got walked out on. Either he was not ready for a commitment, or he just used me. And I pray this isn't another because I truly love you and I do feel strongly about us."

"Lavonia, listen, in two days, we will be married. So, forget all this! Let's eat dinner and prep for Las Vegas."

Now, that innocent smile returns. With trust, we ate and left for home. Home is such a warm feeling, being with the one you love. It's going to be great! I can feel it.

We arrived. We sat on the couch. She laid her head in my lap, looked me in the eyes and said, "God is about to do some wonderful things in the next six months. I can feel it."

She held me close, then she smiled the angel smile that she shares with just the presence of her existence. It was always extravagant. Before long, while listening to The Commodores "Sweet Love," she was asleep again in my arms, peaceful as a newborn baby. I slid her head onto the sofa and covered her beautiful, firm body.

Myself, I went to my new man cave to pray. To thank God for all He's doing and what He's about to do. This was now my spot to chill with the furniture from my old place.

We talked for a while—God and I talked. And I'm sure He was listening because it was very quiet and still. I was just content with the peace. And I fell asleep.

As I slept, I dreamed a dream of money. Money that's going to come when it's needed the most. Money that is ours from God. I was awakened by a kiss on the forehead

from my girl, she knows I was in the man care.

"Baby let's shower and get some sleep. Got a long day ahead."

So, we did. We held each other all through the night. Such a quiet night. With our feet tangled and our toes tingling we drifted off into a peaceful sleep.

The day. We packed the luggage in her SUV, made calls that were important, and off we went to prepare for our destination. Arrived at the airport, boarded. We landed somewhere between the nap. We exit the plane. Lavonia had made all the reservations, including a shuttle at the airport, rooms rented, and dinner invitations. And myself, I didn't know until we arrived at the motel.

When we got to the room, champagne was on ice. There were hors d'oeuvre and a view overlooking the city.

"What a city! It's beautiful, flashing neon lights."
So many people walking to casinos. We sat out on the balcony of our hotel room reminiscing about all good stuff. Not knowing where to begin. It's still early. So, we decided to visit the city of money.

We walked for hours. Mapped out the Justice of the Peace where we will be married tomorrow, and just ate different appetizers on the Sunset Strip while tasting a variety of wines. As more activities arose, we took a carriage ride. We also took pictures for our new photo album of the years we will be sharing together. When it was time, we went in for the night and watched movies until we fell asleep.

The phone rang about six o'clock, it was our wake-upcall. Then the doorbell rang. It was room service. Lavonia had planned everything! She always made sure everything was set, breakfast in bed.

We prayed, ate, and took a shower. Still had hours before we got ready for the most important day of our lives to become one, not just in marriage, but also in the body of Christ.

After breakfast, we found a beach and took a walk, just to chill for the moment.

"Now, it's time to retire to our suite to get dressed."
It wasn't suit and tie. Just nice outfits that matched, and off we went to the Justice of the Peace. Once we arrived, it was people we didn't even know greeting us and attending the wedding. Must have been over 50 people.

Now, it's done. We are married. Then out of the blue, a man walked up and prayed over us. He prophesied that the two of us would come into a lot of money, and that we would know what to do with it. It's our calling, he said. I chilled as something came over me and Lavonia immediately started speaking in tongues. When I looked around for the minister, he was gone!

We held each other close and walked through the door.

The guests, throwing rice as we exit. The limousine was there to take us to another suite. She had it all down packed.

When we arrived, I carried her over the threshold with power. Our luggage was in the center of the room. We danced around for a moment and ended up on the balcony, twelve stories high, and it was beautiful.

We sat there drinking wine with cheese and crackers while eating fruit, looking at all the pictures we had taken since we arrived. So colorful! The wedding pictures looked as if we were meant to be. Then I received a call from Gee, who managed the mobile home park that I owned, now we own. Something about someone wanting to buy three mobile homes.

“Maybe later, bro. Right now, I'm on a business trip. We'll connect later,” I said.

Lavonia and I decided to go downstairs to the Garden Room for dinner. A beautiful Garden Room it was! People were staring at us as though they knew us. Like royalty, just like the night we first dated.

I asked my bride, “What have you planned here?” Didn't know why they were looking at us. We weren’t the only African Americans there, and she had planned nothing because it was my idea to go to dinner.

In the Garden Room, Lavonia looked like a flower that was planted in this garden. People just continued to speak and stare. After dinner, we shot pool at the little spot at the corner of the Sunset Strip. Just an ordinary day but married.

Belonging to someone made the difference in living, and God's blessing was present. There was a big screen at the end of the Strip, an outdoor movie theater. We attended a classic with Bing Crosby. The site was cool to be outside.

It's late. We went to turn in to prepare for another day. Little did she know I had plans of my own for us tomorrow.

We slept through the night, caressed tightly in each other’s arms as one joined as Siamese twins. Morning arrived. A knock at the door; its room service. Breakfast never smelled so good. But this time, as I had planned, we got served by a waiter. She giggled.

This was just the tip of the iceberg. After breakfast, I gave her a massage and fed her fruit. We took a shower and made passionate love. We fell back asleep on a soft rug on the bathroom floor. Slept for three hours without even realizing it. The day was still young, so we decided to shower and take a walk. We walked to this big field for the plans I have for my girl.

"Baby, I must blindfold you. "Not again" she said. I have wanted to do this event for years. Trust me," I said. And she allowed me to. The instructor was aware of what to do. We entered into this box. She's scared.

"What's this, baby? What are you up to now," she asked?

And it lifted slowly. I waited until we were at least 1,000 feet before removing the blindfold.

She cleared her eyes and screamed, "Oh, my god! A hot air balloon!"

I thought that she was scared.

"I've always wanted to do this." I said.

"Me too! Oh, Curtis! You are the greatest!" she said.

After the kisses and hugs, I open up the picnic basket.

On our journey, we viewed for a three-hour tour. Lavonia 's eyes lit up like a Christmas tree--a little kid waiting to see gifts at Christmas. I've never seen her excited in this way. I know that she is pleased and that's important to me.

Once landed, she wanted to go again. “Please, please!”

She sounded like a spoiled kid. I informed her that it was a one trip a day ride.

Now, the time is 6pm in the city that never sleeps. And that's true! What surprised me the most is, Las Vegas has an aquarium and other places I never had a chance to visit in my life and do hope that she will enjoy, open 24 hours.

We walked until we reached the aquarium. Still full of joy, we toured the whole aquarium. Believe it or not, time just seemed to stand still. It actually was late, but it seemed that the evening was still young. We left, stopped to get a drink and dips at our hotel bar. Life is great at this moment. Then went up to go to bed to rest because we're leaving tomorrow going to Warner Robins. We are going to let everyone know we got married. We're going to actually announce it on the 4th of July celebration. No one knows.

Then the phone rang.

"Guess who?"

My brother, Von, just to say hello, how's it going. We talked for a while. He did say the job was in order and that they have set their date for July 10th.

We said our goodbyes.

He stated, "We will see you guys at the 4th of July Celebration."

I called Franklin just to see how it's going.

"Everything's cool, cuz."

"I have a list of 127 people who are supposed to show up. Well, it's going to be a grand time. Hit you up around 12:00 cuz."

Morning meant an early breakfast. Wanted to get back just to relax the day away. We were in Warner Robins without anyone knowing. Not even mother. Just wanted to chill. Lavonia's mom and dad called just to see how's everything, they were not sure will they make it.

"Just fine, Mother." They talked for a moment.

She said, “Hope to see you soon.” Later that day, we checked into a motel, unpacked and relaxed. The day was still a little young, so I asked my wife was there anything she liked to do. Just relax. So, I told her I had a little business to take care of. Go ahead.

“I’m just going to chill.”

I went to meet Franklin. It's a quarter to twelve at The Spot. Everything was going well. It's setup like a family reunion. We talked and just chilled. Then the mentioning of Moncelisa might be coming by your mother's. She asked was you coming to town on the 4th. I told her, don't have any clue. Last I heard, cuz was in Las Vegas. She still got it bad for you. I can see it in her eyes. Subject changed.
Oh, Well! Her lost.

We talked about my announcement. In what order, cuz. He asked continuously about the announcement. What's up, cuz? You got rich? Married? Or, what? You will just have to see. Then we departed. I stopped by Macy's and bought Lavonia a two-piece short pants set because God's angel needs to be represented. I called Von before I retreated to the room. He's on his way down a day early.

“Cool,” I said.

“Just wanted to know where you guys staying. Should be there by 3pm. We can eat dinner.”

“My treat,” I said.

“Oh, yeah. Cool.” He replied.

This will be a good evening and plan. What I mean is, Glo and Von know much of my family. This will give Lavonia company since no one knows her that much. She can hang with Glo until the announcement. I'll let her know. Just introduce her as a friend from Atlanta and move on.

I returned to our room. Gave my baby her gifts, then said, “We're going out tonight around six.”

We sat, watched tv for a while. Then a knock. “Baby, can you get that?”

Von had texted me saying they're in the lobby. He’s sending Glo up. Lavonia answered the door. Surprise! You know how ladies do. Girl, you got to tell me about Las Vegas! And, of course, I left to help Von. We chatted.

“Curt, you are looking good, little brother,” he said.

“And I feel great. Just hope I don't run into the exes. By the way, has Glo talked with Vee lately, or Mona Lisa,” I asked?

“Not sure,” she would have told me, though, cuz.

It is what it is, Von would always say. We walked over to O'Charlie's to shoot pool. We went to the rooms to get prepared for dinner, in which Von liked O'Charlie's, made reservations while we were here. Walking distance. No one must drive. Can't wait until this week is over to return home married for four more days and do nothing. Prep our life and goals, make scrap books, photo albums. Just us, just thinking out loud, so we left for our room.

The hour has come for dinner. We walked to O'Charlies. Chilled at the bar for a while, watching the big screen. Sipping' on wine, snacking' on salsa, just to break out the moment. Just the thing to do to chill. Lavonia and I played darts while Von and his girl shot pool. Late-night dinner, and something different, but it brought joy to another. As the night passed, a light meal with laughter, but joy. After dinner, Lavonia and I decided to just stroll around the mall just to enjoy the rest of the night before turning in after a long day. Tomorrow is going to be with my family to bring aboard my new Queen. Can't wait to see people who I haven't seen in a few years. I know it will be good. Lavonia looked me in my eyes with a sparkle.

"Baby, I'm tired. Let's go in." So, we left for our room; Von and Glo already in. We sat up for a spell just holding each other until we fell asleep watching tv.

The day rose. We walked to IHOP for breakfast. My partner, nowhere in sight. After we ate, we arrived at the hotel. I called Von to let them know we're leaving around 2pm. Everything's good, but just a little tired. Called my cuz, Franklin, just to check in.

"Man! There's about 75 people here," he said.

"See you soon."

So, we all left in one car to go to the 4th of July celebration. We arrived. Glo and Lavonia mingled while Von and I located the table with my family. And I found it. My Shawty looked at me but couldn't tell it was her son because her eyes had gotten bad. I got closer.

"Curtis," she said with a soft yell.

Everyone glanced and greeted. My grandkids, daughters, sons and sons-in-laws were all there. We embraced. They all remember Von and his family. My sister and all the family together were a good feeling. We all just chilled. Then I looked over the crowd where she stood; tall, dark, and lovely as ever. You already know Moncelisa. She was staring at me with anger and bitterness in her eyes, not sure why she's here.

I started walking in her direction. As she notices, she walked away and didn't look back. I thought maybe I could have spoken a word. So, I changed my course. It was about time to make the announcement.

I called Lavonia in to meet us at the area setup for this. My mom, my children all headed in this direction. Franklin called. It's about that time. I gradually seated Mother and met Lavonia at the stage for other activities.

"May I have your attention, please?" I stated.

"It's good for family to get together as planned. Spoke of gratefulness. And now, to introduce a new member. This is Lavonia, my wife."

The center of attention now, everything got quiet for just a moment. Then introductions came about for the ones she did not know. Spoke about our one-day journey. And we all just fell in the crowd. Back to enjoying life. You know how you feel when someone is staring at you. And it was true!

Moncelisa, now with the look that could kill. I just stood there like puzzled as she gritted her teeth and rolled her eyes. I walked away in a totally different direction. The day was long. Mother wanted to go in. So, Lavonia, Glo and my girls took her home. Before she left, she said to stop by before I leave Warner Robins. We hugged, said our love, and she left. Von and I chilled a little while longer.

Everyone congratulated me on the catch out of heaven because Lavonia is beautiful. We just hung out because the celebration was about to end plus Lavonia needed to clean up after spilling juice on her pants. We hung around for a few hours. Lavonia and Glo called, said they're going back to the room. And I said to be safe. We cleaned up. I showed a little love for the ones who helped put this 4th of July celebration together. They were grateful.

Von and I left to go and shoot some pool and to talk. Little Bro, God is so good. We just talked, left and went to the motel. Getting late. My wife and I decided to just get to sleep so that we can prepare for tomorrow to visit Mother and return to Alpharetta.

The morning rose. We all ate at the IHOP, reminiscing on the celebration when people got together to chill and all enjoyed the moment. Like I said, it was good to see everyone together once again, and this time, not a funeral.

We walked back to the motel to check out. Von and

Glo left. My baby and I took a drive to Mother's. She asked that I stop by before leaving.

“Son,” she said. “It’s a good thing that you helped bring the family together. We're not getting younger. But the reason why I asked you to stop by was I need $500.00, and please don't ask why like your brother does. Even when he gives me $30.00, he wants to know what the hell I’m going to do with it."

“I didn’t ask. And, I wasn't going to ask,” She

said.

“I understand if you don't have it. But I need it in two

weeks.”

“Fine, Mother. Soon as we get back to Alpharetta, I’ll send it.”

Mother said, “Thank you!”

I asked for her account number so that I could just deposit it tomorrow.

“I'll call you when it's there.”

Some kind of way, Lavonia must have done what they call “ear hustling” because ten minutes later, she approached us and said, “Mother Jewell, it's done.”

I'm looking for her, saying, “What's done?”

"The money has been transferred."

Now I'm thinking ESP! Nothing was said or discussed.

"That's a good woman, son, don't mess it up," my mother said.

"Oh, no, Mother. That's my mate." I said.

Then she asked, "Did you see Moncelisa at the picnic?"

"Yes," I answered, but she walked away as I approached her.

"Didn't get a chance to speak. I know she's angry even more now that I didn't marry her. All I want to do is be her friend."

"Just stay clear, son."

"Okay, Mother. We're going to leave. Got things to do." We left.

We decided to stop by the Apostolic Church where my pastor resides to introduce my wife and to let him know that I'll be visiting from time to time. But now, I'm thinking about V-Lisa and how's she going to take it because I didn't marry her either, or Glo, as her friend. She never told her because pastor spoke to me in person, stated that she was engaged and now I'm relieved. We said our goodbyes. Pastor prayed over us, and we left to start our journey to Atlanta. I was tired. So, Lavonia drove.

I relaxed, just thinking of the wife God set forth for me. She's brilliant and she loves God. But most of all, she got my back in the best interests.

We arrived at home, relaxed. Prepping for work, since the honeymoon and 4th of July is now over with. Time to prep for work all over again. The day was over. We ate dinner and around seven, then we just went to sleep.

Six months had passed.

Von and Glo Wedding

On to enjoy their new life, new home, and new born;

Everything was going as God planned by faith, I'd like to think. So again, I say Lavonia and I grew much closer and fortunate. One day, Lavonia called me and asked that I come home for lunch.

"Sure, why not?"

Hot love at mid-day. Still burning desires. I reached my front door, waiting for Lavonia to greet me with a smile. A different smile. We ate lunch, and there was no rush. She walked behind me and put her hand over my eyes. Not expecting blind sex today. At least, that's what I'm thinking. But when I opened my eyes to focus on the table on a plate, as a servant delivers a message to his master,
there's a thick envelope in front of me. It says Invent Help.

"Come on! Open it," she says anxiously!

But the look in her eyes said she felt good about this mail.

"Come on, baby. Open it." Exiting and rushing!

I open the letter slowly that was certified. Read two pages and then suddenly without a push, I fell out of my chair to the floor.

She said, "Curtis, what is it?"

And again, I fell to the floor on my knees holding the

letter in the air to heaven where it came from. I couldn't speak. I began to just cry. I rolled around on the floor. I looked to my wife who stood smiling with hands folded in desperation. What was she thinking? She must've thought I was crazy! She should have been the one that I was holding, but instead, it was the Lord I embraced. My eyes pleaded for comfort from her, and like the beautiful person she is, all she said was, "What, baby?"

So, I gave her the letter. She read three pages and joined me on the floor. Praying and screaming, "It's a miracle! We were prophesied this on our wedding day."

I knew I had discussed the invention and patent for the invention with her a year ago, but now it was being developed and purchased for 12.5 million dollars!

"Yes! Now, I know that God has delivered what visions He had for us. 12.5 million dollars.

I'm thinking what to do with the money, and what to do about working. I called in sick. Lavonia was still on vacation this week. We sat and held each other for the rest of the day. We couldn't stop the tears of joy.

We started planning. First, we're going to need an attorney to handle our affairs. My brother, Wayne, came to my mind. He recently received a degree and had opened his office in Macon, Georgia. I looked up the office number to set an appointment. Lavonia agreed.

This was Monday, and the appointment was set for Tuesday at 3pm. I told Lavonia, "Baby, I got to go by the office to put in a two weeks' notice." I asked what she was going to do.

"I'm a nurse, baby. I must continue my work. God will direct us."

I didn't oppose to her quitting because I know God has plans for this. We agreed not to spread the word. I needed to tell somebody. But who? I called my cousin, Johnny, who will take part in this fortune. Just as life was to go for me, it was game, set and match, and I won. But did I?

Man, this is great! I went into my man cave. I just sat there and started talking to God, asking Him what is it that He wants me to do. Hours, I sat waiting on an answer. nothing.

I left to go into the office. Talked to my boss and explained He blessed me, and I left. I will be by in a week to clean out my office. I looked for my brother, Von, but not around. But left him a message to call me. Von is my ace. I left the office to visit the park in which I haven't been in a while. Again, to talk with God on what to do. The thing I've learned is not to rush. I decided to leave because it's about dinner time and I don't want to miss my wife's cooking. A great Southern cook she is. I arrived home.

She looked in my eyes and said, "Give God time, baby."

It's as if she's in my thoughts. It's the ways we connect as one. I felt eased at this time. We sat down for dinner, prayed, ate. What a meal! Then we sat out on our patio enjoying the night air, writing notes about plans to discuss with my brother, Wayne tomorrow and Johnny.

It's late. We took a bath together, and off to bed we went. When morning arrived, we ate breakfast and took our morning walk. Lavonia asked to take a shower before lunch. Maybe the desires of intimacy were on both our minds. Again, no. After the shower, she took me by the hand, guided me to our office in the back of the house. She showed me seven pictures of office space buildings. Sometime during the night, she worked on this. Like I said before, she's the one that helps make my life complete. She had already setup three appointments.

"Thank you, baby," I said with a kiss, and then the phone rang. It was my cousin, Johnny. I told him I needed to meet with him at 3:00 at my brother's office, and to please be there.

He asked, "Is everything okay?"

"Couldn't be better, cuz," I told him.

"Sure, I'll meet you," he said. Little did he know, he's about to be asked to become our financial adviser. We hung up, and off Lavonia and I went to our appointments.

We received three places to buy for the location for our office and off to Macon, Georgia we went to meet Wayne and Johnny. We had time to stop to see Mother, a surprise visit. She was glad to see us. Lavonia and my niece talked while Mother wanted me to take her somewhere. To talk. Then she brought up Moncelisa, saying she's very angry about how I walked out of her life completely, she still confused, it's over.

" Be very careful, son?" Second time she asked.

She seemed disturbed. That's not unusual for Moncelisa. We talked for a while. I gave her $400.00 without asking. She felt my forehead.

"Son. You okay?"

“Yes mother I’m fine.”

“You never gave me $400.00,” she said.

“Mother, I love you. And I’m happy.”

“I can see that!” She smiled.

Off from her place we went to pick up my wife. I walked up to my niece, Tay, I call her. Gave her a hug and an envelope. Asked her not to open it until her birthday. If she's going to wait, it has $500.00 in it. Apparently, she didn't open it. I got no call. Her birthday was 8 days away. I left her an envelope that for my niece Erika that contain the same thing.

We left for Wayne's office. Johnny was there. I greeted him and gave him the letter from Invent Help. He spun around in his chair like a kid on a merry-go-round.

“Bro, God has truly blessed your family!”

“Cuz, read it,” he said, “Cisco, you the man.”

That's my nickname. Cuz always called me this. I explained I'm not sure of God's plans, but you guys are involved.

“Bro, I need you as my attorney,” I told Wayne.

“Cuz, I need you as my financial consultant,” I said to Johnny.

"Anything you need, we will be there," Wayne said.

"I need guidance, bro, and a will. We're looking at opening an office in Atlanta. By the first of the month, we should be in one. So, I will keep you posted. Send $25,000.00 to this account. Talk with the owner who owns the house Mother lives in and buy it. I promised her years ago I would buy her a house.

"I need this like last year!"

I told him. "Cuz, I need you to help me with the finances. Not sure what yet, but it's coming. I want to visit my girls before I get back to Alpharetta. So, I'm gonna get out of Alpharetta. We will be in touch in a few days."

We said our goodbyes and off we went. The phone rang. It was my brother, Von, finally returning my call from a recent message. I should have told him over the phone, but he might be driving and lose focus. So, I will just see him later.

It was getting late, and I was going to visit my girls and my grands. We haven't seen them since the Fourth of July celebration. We arrived at Amethyst's home at dinner time. She, and her three girls, Kiannaa, Aylisa, Mykala, and Mike were about to eat dinner.

We were asked to join but said no since it wasn't going to be a long visit. We talked a while, and off we went to Macon to visit Nicki and her four girls and son: Brianna, Ayinah, Arion Akedea and AJ. Always Kool-Aid to visit family, especially when we do not live close. It's getting late. It's really time to get back to Alpharetta. Got a lot to do tomorrow. So, we said our goodbyes, and off we went.

The next day was spent doing more office-shopping to decide on a space. I let Lavonia take charge of this project because, today, I'm going to clean out my office, and talk with my boss and Von. Who's taking my position? I arrived at the job. Went by Von's office, and he was in. We talked, and I invited him and Glo over for dinner. Then, I went upstairs to the boss. He was glad to see me, since he knew of the fortune I received, but not the amount. He had already given the position to Von, but he didn't know at the time. We chatted more, and off I went.

Lavonia called to meet for lunch at the Varsity. I stopped by the bank to open an account, then went to meet her. I gave her a bank card with unlimited funds to do whatever she needed. We enjoyed lunch, then she went to meet Glo. I returned home to prepare dinner. Something light, not too heavy. I decided to take a short nap since we had company coming by at 7:00.

Lavonia had come home unexpectedly, and I was asleep in the living room in her favorite chair. Don't know how long she'd been there. When Von and Glo arrived, we ate dinner, and then, I told them the news about the $12.5 million. They were ecstatic. I told Von about what's about

to happen. That where God gave me the course to take, he's in it. We all went out to the patio.

Von kept repeating, "$12.5 million! My little buddy paid; God paid off, your work Bro."

The night was about to be over, so we said our goodbyes. Lavonia and I took a shower and went to bed.

Two weeks passed without a course from God on what to do with our fortune. So, I decided to call Pastor Fogarty, to set an appointment because I needed guidance seeking for answers. He accepted for an hour. I called my wife to let her know that I was driving to Warner Robins and would return in about four hours.

"Do you want to travel with me?" I asked.

She stated that she's very busy. So, I went on. Called a bro of mine from the church I attended in Atlanta to see if he'd ride with me, and he agreed. I picked him up and we headed south. Never told him about my fortune, just a regular visit, hanging out with a brother. We arrived at the church in Warner Robins, and I talked to the pastor about the fortune and how to pay tithes from it, and any ministries he can give me on the answers I'm waiting on from God. Patience is the only word he gave.

I called my brother to forward a check for tithes for $10,000 to the church and told the pastor to expect it soon. I didn't want to spend a lot of time in Warner Robins, but I did visit some family. Of course, I had to visit my little Shawty. It's always good to be with mother my nieces and sister. I cut her grass, cleaned up, and off we went back to Atlanta.

My brother called and stated he bought the house that she lived in, and I knew to prepare a family dinner for the dedication. Just aunts and a few friends. I'll get one of the members to put this together. She's going to be very happy. Tears of joy poured down my face. It's something I told me mother. That someday I will buy her a house, and it's done. To give her the deed will be exciting! This was only the work of the Lord. We arrived in Atlanta.

I stopped by Steak-n-Shake to get a bite to eat. I wanted to tell Jerry about my fortune, but I didn't. I dropped him off and I went home. Before I got home, Lavonia called, gave me an address to meet her. She said to drive around the back enter to throw the back door.

Not knowing what she's up to, I arrived in an empty parking lot. Came through the back door of a building. Surprise! People jumped out surprising Lavonia grabbed me and walked me through the little crowd of people that I knew.

“What's going on, baby?” I asked.

She blindfolded me and led me outside the building, but through the front. Then, off came the blindfold, and there, it read 'TPS & Associates' in big lettering. I'm standing astonished, overwhelmed, and speechless! She gave me an envelope. It was the deed to our office. I knew she was up to something these few weeks. Instead of her enjoying her vacation, she's busy building dreams. That's another reason why I love her; unpredictable.

She showed me around. Showed me my office. It's very nice. She has furnished everything, and the phone was even on. My business number that I have had for years. She out did it herself, but it's a course that God led her to do. Now, my question is what to do with an office. Still no answer from God.

We popped the champagne, while a caterer served. Then she peeled the label that said TPS & Associates, President, Curtis E. Turner. In my office, my name is engraved, and to top it off, she had designed the wall in my office. It was all family, all the children, grands, Mother, and us.

I thanked her with a kiss. Asked her to pray with me. In this building, we prayed. She left me alone as if I asked her to. I was about to. It's like she knew. She went to host the guests while I sat in my chair at my desk. What a beautiful view! Staring out at a big tree. That, just looking out my window, made the moment complete. Squirrels running around. Chirping birds. Seemed so peaceful. I spent about an hour in my new office praying for the purpose. I just sat there relaxed, stress free of a new beginning.

I called my cuz, Johnny, who was my financial consultant. I asked if he would setup a payment plan of one thousand dollars a month to send to my daughters, five hundred to send to my mother, and five hundred for my sister and nieces. He asked if, I was sure. I told him I was very sure, and that I also needed to open trust funds for the grands, with an allowance of one hundred dollars a week.

"That's a lot of funds, cuz!" Johnny said.

"Don't worry, cuz, I said, God has a plan to put it all back. I'm sure, cuz." Preparing for the family future. No one knows what's about to happen.

I decided to call my aunts to help me give Mother a surprise dinner party. Just a few friends from her church and a few family members so that we could give her the ultimate surprise and present her with the deed to her home. It was done and it's this week.

The gathering is only three days from now, and we have a lot of work to do, but it will happen. I called Johnny to forward some funds over to my daughter Amethyst. She enjoys doing these kinds of things and she has the time to do it. She set the surprise dinner up and asked everyone not to talk about it. When the day of the gathering arrived, I asked my brother to just take mom out for the day, so we could get everything set up. He returned around seven, and when he drove into the driveway, Mom knew something was up. Little did she know, there was more to it. She asked

Wayne what was going on and was everything ok. My brother told her yes and to relax.

She entered her home, and Surprise! Family she hadn't seen in some time now came to greet her, and she just started crying. What's going on, it's okay mother. A couple of hours into the celebration it was time to dedicate this moment to our mother. No one knew about the deed.

I asked for silence, and said, "Mother, we love you, and I want you to know that your son has been blessed. I know I said someday I would buy you a house. So, Mother, here is the deed to your house."

She began to cry with a scream, "Where is this house?"

Everyone was speechless and mumbling. "Mother, this is your house," I said.

She hugged her sons and daughter. "Thank you, God, for my children," she said.

"Thank you for this house."

We gave her a check for $5,000.00. More tears.

"Now, you can buy new furniture, if you wish."

Everyone applauded and congratulated her. It was getting late, and family began leaving. Lavonia and I stayed the night, and in the morning, we said our goodbyes and left for Alpharetta. Lavonia and I needed some of our time together. We went shopping at the Farmer's Market.

We decided to go out to dinner at New Orleans Seafood and enjoy the rest of the day. Afterwards, we ended up at the park where we used to visit, the one where we fell in love. This was a beautiful park, we used to visit all the time. Then, it hit me. I started speaking in tongues. I fell to my knees. "That's it! That's it!" I screamed. People in the park ran over to see what's going on. Is he okay do?

Lavonia said, "He's okay. God just delivered his answer." She knew.

She knew it was a breakthrough. "That's it, b," I said.

"What do you mean, honey?"

"Let's go home. I'll explain later," I said.

We arrived home, poured a glass of wine and toasted to patience.

Children Out of Israel was a project God gave us a few years ago to open a community development center throughout Georgia. Since she dealt with kids, I explained to her how important the program was to God and how it needed her guidance.

"That's wonderful, baby. You're going to need a strong, devoted team of saints to build this vision. Tomorrow we will start building the umbrella for TPS & Associates. Everything is falling into God's plan and season again. I asked my wife what she is going to do about her job.

"Baby, I'm still waiting on God." she said.

Nothing else was said. We showered and went off to bed. Guess what? This night intimacy was on the menu. We slept until 1:30 in the afternoon without knowing it was that late. What the hell, we can do this now. Why rush the clock to get to work for no money, but for God's Grace.

We finally got up and gratefully cooked breakfast at 2 am. Breakfast is always a good meal. Started discussing the Children of Israel. She's listening and writing notes. I'm talking, laying it down as if God is speaking through me. I felt He was laying out His plans only for my wife, my partner, my mate, to put everything in perspective, and for me to have patience with her results. I explained how I wanted to take part and the purpose. Nothing else was needed. I told her that I would leave you full control over this matter.

"The hiring, the salary, it's 'your call," I said.

She said thanks and she went to the office. I left to visit my brother, Von, to tell him that whatever he needed, I had him. If you need a better job, it's yours. He said, “Little bro, I'm content with my new job, but I do need a new set of wheels.”

I wrote Von a check for thirty-thousand dollars. He’s not questioning the money. “Bro, take it, it's yours,” I said.

We hugged as brothers, chatted a little more. Then, I told him where my office was, to stop by after work, and off I went. Stopped at the Varsity to get a bite, then went to the office. I was just looking out the window at God's creations and thanking Him for peace. As I sat staring at the oddly shaped oak tree outside my office window, a strange feeling came over me. I was sitting here resting on good fortune. A fortune that I had not shared with my brothers, remembering promises made when we were younger and hitting myself for forgetting this important detail. A snap decision was made, and I set up a meeting with my brothers for the following weekend at Smokes' in Warner Robins, that place holds many enduring memories for us all. In addition, we all agreed that no one else was to know of my arrival. the day came to visit.

As I stepped out of my car into the parking lot of Smoke's, a warm feeling came over me. I was about to see the brothers I haven't seen over 7 years. I ordered a beer and started walking around the place. The only thing that had changed were the people. Everything else was somewhat the same. I looked at the old pool table and was amazed. It still had the name I carved on it before leaving Warner Robins. CISCO!! Wow!! That table had seen many battles between my brothers and I. Most of them I won, or I like to think so.

"You can't go back," a voice rang out in the near distance.

I stopped in my tracks. A huge smile found its way to my face. I anticipated turning around. Was that my youngest brother I am hearing? I turned up my beer and sat the bottle on the pool table, and every so slowly did I turn. Then there was the explosion. Thick as thieves, the brother's four were together again. There was laughter, joking, and a lot of horsing around. For old time's sake, we shot a few games of pool.

When the time came for us to start getting serious, we found a table in the corner of the bar and ordered drinks. I spoke to them of my success, but only in small portions. I did not tell them how far I was going with the ideas but did include how I wanted them to be a part of what I was doing. They all listened with such ease; each with their own questions. Somehow, I kept looking at Elliot. I remembered how smart he was with numbers, and out of the brothers, he was my first choice. I offered him a job that brought about his hesitation because he no longer lived in Georgia.

"How could he explain to his family that he was to be my accountant? Would they be willing to relocate to Atlanta?"

He asked for a couple of days and sweetened the pot to keep him speedily to make the decision, a couple of days to discuss with the family he said.

My company would pay for relocation, housing, and a handsome salary. As for the rest, they were happy just to receive the check that I placed in their hands. Each was given a part and share in the company, and after their acceptance, I felt complete. I have kept my thoughts on what would one do with a million bucks. Just as I slipped into Warner Robins, I slipped out and back home to my wife.

As I arrived home, Lavonia was waiting at the door. The greeting was one I did not expect but gave all the reasons why I married her. She told me that Elliot had called the office number and for me to set everything up. Then she looked at me strangely, and just like a woman, she did not say a word. After talking to Elliot, arrangements were made for him and his family to relocate to Georgia, and my company had an accountant. He had two months to relocate from Seattle Washington to Atlanta Georgia.

Two months had passed, and Lavonia had built a team of 12 to begin TPS & Associates. I don't know how, when she is working a full-time job, but she did it. Everything is in working order, and all I do is dictate what's required and she takes care of the staffing. One night while Lavonia and I were just relaxing and watching tv, she said, "Baby, I may resign. I'm stunned!"

"You're going to need me," she said.

"Yes, baby. I do." "Everything you have Curtis, comes from God. I will help you make it happen. I love you."

She kissed me on the forehead with a smile.

Everything is in its proper channels now. I can focus on God's projects.

With the business expanding and the demand for hiring more people increasing, I had one such person in mind. As I told you before, my relationship with Moncelisa was a sick one. And I still had a twinge of care for her. I went against everything my wife warned me about and hired her as the executive director of TPS & Associates. She turned out to be what I needed to run this company. She was bright, smart and a brilliant help worker. My wife did not agree with my decision. As I believed, it was because of a wife and jealous of the ex-thing, but that was far from the truth. Lavonia simply did not trust her, period. That's a women intuition, but she accepted the trust in me.

This went on for more than two years. When Moncelisa requested the hiring of two students, I agreed, but the responsibility for training them rested on her shoulders. As usual, she did a great job and the students proved to be better than I imagined. Desiree and Dre were students from Fort Valley State College, they worked a little more than two years when Moncelisa became ill, causing her to resign. Desiree took her place. As part of our company policy, Moncelisa was financially settled and had no needs to worry about anything. One month later management brought to my attention that something was wrong with the books. Six-hundred thousand dollars was not accounted for, and there was no trace of where the money went. No receipts, and no clues. I decided to call Desiree, who was now my executive director, and set up meetings. He had no clue as to what it was about. To me, it was all about the element of surprise. I would get all the records needed without giving her a chance to fix things and Elliot would locate where the money went. The perfect plan was set into motion. The only thing left was time.

In the meantime, Lavonia came to me. She wanted to share in this part of my life. I did not want her to give up her nursing career. So, together we decided she would work part-time. Without knowing it, she became the foundation. The main support that I needed to make this plan of God's work.

Together we came up with the idea to start a prayer service movement across the nation. This included a prayer box set throughout cities where all people can request prayer for whatever their circumstances were.

We emptied the boxes each week and prayed over them. Just like the sayings of old who gave animals for sacrifices, these prayers went up as a sacrifice to the Lord. This ordeal made headlines, which meant more money for the organization to build visions.

It was now close to the time of our meeting with Desiree. When I received a phone call to come to Crawford-Long Hospital, nothing else was said. I didn't know what was going on, but the word "hospital" made me jump and move. Lavonia met me at the emergency room door, her head held down. I grabbed and examined her to make sure she was all right, then I held her close and thanked God she was not the reason for my being there. Without words, she led me to a room where a serious-looking man stood. He introduced himself as Detective Bynum.

No more words were spoken. I was just led to a table that was covered with pictures. One look. That was all it took. I looked to my wife, then at the detective. I didn't recognize anything. So, I asked loudly what the hell was going on. No answer was given. My frustration was building, and that was when Lavonia put her hand on my shoulder as Detective Bynum held a photo before me.

I looked at it for a moment. Then, as I picked it up, familiarity set in. Elliot. Elliot! I shook the thoughts as

Lavonia held on to me. Even though we were not brothers by blood, we were brothers through life circumstances. Thick as thieves, we were brothers. As reality showed its ugly face, I screamed louder than I knew
I could.

I could not hear what the detective was saying. I couldn't hear my wife. I couldn't even hear my own thoughts. Just as a bull in the rodeo who sees a red cape, my mind imploded and ventured into the valley of the Red Sea.

“Who did this?” was my question to Detective Bynum.

His answer was a robbery gone bad after more questioning, I found out that Elliot had eighteen hundred dollars still in his pocket along with a business card that carried the name of TPS & Associates.

How could this be a robbery when the only thing that was taken was a watch and briefcase? The cab driver was not hurt at all, and his account of the events did not match up. Something was dead wrong! The only description of the suspect given was a six-foot, five black male who
drove off in a black Lexus. My mind flowed like a river. How can I tell family and friends? Lavonia agreed to be the

messenger and decide for his family to arrive. This alone freed up some of my time, leaving me room to investigate. Four days passed, and still no answer. Nothing to go on. We buried my brother on November 11th, and after one month, there were no new leads and the case was closed, until anything else showed up.

One evening, I received a phone call from Mrs. Hickey, Elliot's wife. As I listened to her words about a large sum of money not accounted for. She said Elliot was on his way to see me. Steam blew from my nostrils! I was never given a message that Elliot wanted to see me! This whole situation was getting stranger by the minute, and I knew it was time to act. What could I do? My mind was on a mental freak. A whirling roller coaster going up slowly only to come down fast. I knew it was time for me to plan my move.

I hired a private investigator named Mike White and a new accountant, gave them their instructions and swore them to secrecy. They were to only talk to me. A few weeks later, Mike White contacted me about his findings. There were over five-hundred thousand dollars missing from several accounts and a very clever thief in God's organization. I called detective Bynum and reported my findings. The phone records showed that Elliot had called the office several days prior to his death, but the trail went cold after that.

With the assistance of Detective Bynum, I called a corporate meeting with all the employees. Some of them were curious. Others were confused. But I had the perfect set up to figure out which employees I can trust.

“Okay, people. I know most of you are wondering why this meeting was called.” I said, looking around at the 20 or so employees.

“Some of you I know. Most of you, I don't. So, for the moment, let's get to know each other.”

Some of the employees were squirming in their seats. Detective Bynum was instructed to take notes on what he observed.

“After looking over your files, I realize some of you are missing a statewide background check. As head of this company, this is a requirement for you to continue to be employed here.”

All the employees looked around the conference room wondering who it was that did not do the background check. I looked around the room, searching for those I knew by their records were most faithful. I only came up with seven. Those seven, I told to meet me in my office. As for the rest, a consent form for a background check was given to them. Some sneered, making it seem like they had something to hide. But which ones? I had to rely on detective Bynum for the answers and decided to let him hire a second detective on more people because this will be a background check to remember. No stone is to be unturned.

After returning to my office, I gave them 7 employees two weeks' vacation time with pay. Some of them asked why. Others just accepted with a smile. After three weeks of background checking, nothing showed up.

Now, it was time to look at the seven that I gave the vacation time to. The main two that piqued my curiosity were the two students. There was something vaguely familiar about them, but I couldn't put my finger on it.

One day, my cousin, Franklin, called asking for a job. Immediately hired him and explained what was going on in the company. After several weeks of working for TPS & Associates, he had to rush home to West Palm Beach because his brother was shot. He saw the students, Dre and

Desiree, on the same plane and I asked Franklin to follow them, if he had time, once at airport.

Franklin decided to call ahead to the hospital and was informed that his brother was in stable condition. So, he sat back and waited to see what the two students' next move was. A black rented Lexus pulled up to where the students were standing, and a black six-foot, five-inch male stepped out with a woman by his side. The two of them were greeted with hugs Franklin informed me he had written down the license number before the car pulled off.

Once again, my mind went into a tailspin. Who were these people? Anyway, Franklin had gotten the address from the rental company and staked out the beach house for several days. Finally, the same man driving the Lexus pulled into the driveway with another car following. Franklin noted that the car was just purchased off the dealer's floor and was driven by none other than Desiree, now I am thinking who?

“I have a strange feeling about this. Now I am in questioning."

“Are Desiree and Dre related, lovers, or what?”

His words caught my attention. What was more surprising is, he said an unfamiliar woman joined them? I immediately sent the private investigators to Florida. Maybe there they could dig up the information that had been puzzling my brain. Who are these students? So far, the only information he found was the students had different last names, Desiree Coley and Dre Tall. But what was their connection? The investigator was playing on a hunch he had and found the name of the man who owns the house, Mike Fry, but he could find no new information without further digging. Meanwhile, the private investigator in Atlanta checked the rest of the staff, but nothing new surfaced, so I called them back to work.

This was becoming a real mystery to me, along with a constant nagging in the back of my head and my mind was forcing me to think: What am I missing? I called human resources and had the employee files of Dre and Desiree brought to my office. It had to find a clue. Franklin stayed in Florida while his brother recovered. He rented the beach house next door to Mike Fly. He continued digging for answers along with the private investigator. Suddenly, just for a brief moment, a spark of hope. The private investigator discovered the name of the two students' mother, La Vita Salo. Yet, it turned out to be another dead end. There was no more information on her. Coming to the end of my rope, I called Dre and Desiree back in to work. That way, I could keep a better eye on them, very suspicious.

Months have passed and we are no closer to finding my brother's killer than we were the day it all began. Everything was set into place. Franklin notice entrance in and out of the beach house. My Atlanta private investigator was checking public records. With my brother's killer heavy on my mind, I neglected my personal life.

My wife, my beautiful wife, Lavonia, had been so patient with me. I received a call from Crawford-Long Hospital with news of my wife collapsing. Terrified was the only emotion I could feel. Lavonia is my life. I would die if anything happened to her. Arriving at the hospital, Pete my number one man and brother, met me at the emergency room door. The Doctor arrived, Mr. Turner.

“Your wife suffered from a low blood count. That, along with the pregnancy and the fatigue, caused her to collapse.”

I was shocked by what the Doctor said! A baby! I am going to be a father, and we never knew about sickle cell.

"Where is she, doc?" I said, without waiting for an answer.

I just ran in the direction he had pointed. Lavonia lying on the bed. The only thing I could think of was wanting to hold her close and reassure her that I am here. The doctor explained about her sickle cell and the need for bed rest. I sat beside Lavonia 's bed, erasing all of the days that labored my brain and concentrating only on her and our unborn child, a call from Family.

Back in Florida, Franklin had found something that might be of interest and called Detective Bynum at Atlanta Metro Police, Detective Bynum flew to Florida because my brother's death was one case that he had to close the book on, but he knew, I needed him.

"Hey, Franklin. What do you have for us?"

"There have been some strange things going on for the past few days. Strange people in and out. There is this one room that is always locked. I have watched Mike Fry unlock it going in and going out. No one else has entered. I can't say for sure if there is probable cause, but I think it's worth checking out."

"What are you saying, man? You think I should get a search warrant?"

"This is exactly what I'm saying, but I couldn't get it myself." He said.

Mike Fry has been gone for three days. A search warrant was issued, and a stakeout was in place. The only thing left was the waiting game. Around 6:00am Saturday morning, Mike Fry returned home. The federal marshal was at his heel with a search warrant in hand. It was not unusual that the officer knew exactly which room to look in; it had a pad lock. About that time the news made it to me, Mike Fry was arrested on person of interests. What was found in his home was over one-hundred thousand dollars, a gun that matches the one used in my brother's murder but can't say it's the weapon or the money.

Finally, some answers. I took a pause after talking to Detective Bynum, thanking him for not giving up. Yet, there were still questions that I needed answers to. My mind started going over the clues. Dre and Desiree had connection with Mike Fry. With them still in my employment, I was determined to find out.

Mike Fry was expedited back to Atlanta, Georgia for questioning. This gave me enough time to make sure Lavonia was safe and felt protected. I had explained to her everything that was going on and she assured me that she would be okay by herself. I still left Pete with her.

It was time to end this and find out what was really going on I decided to go into the office and confront Dre and Desiree about Mike Fry, only to be informed that two of my employees had turned in their resignations. I did not bother to find out who it was I already had a clue. Detective Bynum called me into his office to discuss Mike Fry after looking at him through the two-way mirror.

“I know him, Detective. I know this dude. He's from my hometown!”

Fury turned into anger, which turned into rage! The only vision I saw was me and Mike Fry going into combat with each other. Still, there is that all-important question, "Why? Why did he have to kill my brother? Or did he have any involvement? Something just not right."

Detective Bynum went into question Mike Fry. “Mr. Fry, you know the briefcase and gun that were found in your home was stolen in a robbery and murder case.”

There was no answer.

"Where did you get the briefcase? When was the last time you were in Atlanta," Detective Bynum asked?

"I need to talk to a lawyer. I don't have to answer any more of your damn questions." Fry said.

Detective Bynum came out of the interrogation room. I asked, "Did he tell you how he knew Elliot? Did he say why he killed him?"

"I'm sorry, Curtis once he asked for a lawyer, I had to stop the questioning."

My mind was running rampant.

"How did he know Elliot was coming to Atlanta on that day? Was it a setup? What was my brother coming to tell me?"

This whole thing stinks, and even though we are close to the answer, we are still far away. A call was coming in from my brother, Gee.

"Hello!" I screamed into the phone.

"There's a woman here who is interested in buying the mobile home park. What do you think?"

"Absolutely, not! I will call you back later." I told him.

Really taking care of business. I talked to my wife, who

was going back to her hometown to visit her mother. Detective Bynum told me that warrants were issued for Dre and Desiree. So far, they could not be found. He also stated that my brother's murder was an inside job, and we must find out who the woman was at the beach house. A call came in from the Bureau. They had a match on the set of fingerprints lifted at the beach house.

The prints came back. Moncelisa Brown. Can you believe that? My ex-lover, the very one that wanted her freedom. Why was she out to get me? Suddenly, it hit me hard. Mike Fry, Moncelisa's lover sometime back.

“What did I do to her that was so wrong that she had my brother killed? And to plot this madness."

Reality was beginning to set in. I need to call my mother and warn her. Moncelisa just live a few miles away. Oh, my God! What kind of monster has crawled into her
soul?

Panic had set in so hard that I did not hear Detective
Bynum when he spoke.

“Mr. Curtis, we put an APB out on one Moncelisa Brown.”

I turned to look at Detective Bynum. What was he saying? My mind was in a tailspin. Nothing made sense to me anymore. Moncelisa had access to all the bank accounts, codes. Damn! How can I be so blind and stupid? Now I'm thinking my wife is going to kill me. She had already warned me. And if she was in this, I'll never live up to the pain I brought to my family.

The shrill of my cell phone interrupted my thoughts.

"Gee, what's going on?"

"Ms. LaVita Salo wants to meet with you."

"Ms. Salo, why is her name so familiar to me, Gee? And why does she want to meet with me?"

"She's the one who wants to acquire the mobile home park."

"No, there's something else. That name. It's that name, Gee. Set up the appointment and call me back. If you can get a picture, that would be great."

"All right, boss." I turned and looked at Detective Bynum.

"That was my right-hand man, Gee. He mentioned a Ms. Salo. Is that name familiar to you at all?"

Detective Bynum pondered, “Salo. Salo. That's the mother of those kids, Desiree and Dre, isn't it?”

“Desiree and Dre were another mystery. What the hell is going on, Detective Bynum?”

He said, “Set up the appointment. Find out what her story is. I will have my men set you up with a wire.”

“Sounds like a plan.” I called Gee and had him set up the appointment.

“Wow! Am I going to finally find the answer to my questions, or is this woman just another mystery? Another false lead?”

The meeting was set, and I was told her persistence was great. Now, its time to prepare for the meeting.

I stepped into the restaurant, wired up, and not knowing who I was looking for. Then I remembered Gee saying, “Look for the yellow rose in her hair.”

That's not too hard to spot. I looked and looked. Then my eyes fell upon a vision with a yellow rose. I had to compose myself because baby was looking good. I walked to where she was sitting and introduced myself.

“Are you Ms. Salo?”

“Sit your ass down” she said, pointing a gun at me.

Shocked, I looked at this pretty princess and thought: "Hell, no!"

That's when it happened. She shot me. Pain raced through my shoulder and then through my mind. I wanted to grab her and snatch a knot in her ass, but she had the gun, and she called the shots now.

"Sit your ass down," she repeated!

A bullet to the shoulder. A gun pointed at my head. What else was there to do? I sat down, rubbing my shoulder from the pain. Didn't know what was going on.

"Do you know me? Do you know who I am? Look hard, you son-of-a-bitch!" I knew those words, and that voice Moncelisa used in the past.

I looked at her, wrenching in pain, but I could not tell who she was dizzy. I grabbed my chest and prayed that the wire was working.

"I don't know you. I'm just here to talk about the sale of my mobile home park, and believe me, I hope that you are not the buyer."

Suddenly, as if playing a starring role in the movie Mission Impossible, she pulled off her wig and her face soon followed. I'm looking at Moncelisa indecisive.

“What the hell do you think you're doing?”

“I told you I was going to get back at you.” She said, lowering the gun that brought attention to our table. Mind over matter.

“We're shooting a movie, but no cameras.”

She smirked at the group of onlookers. Only in America, I thought. Where a man can get shot in public and it goes ignored. The onlookers nodded and went back to their usual business. Actually, it was like we were filming a movie but there were no cameras. WHAT THE HELL! Finally they got up and ran out fearful!

“What is wrong with you?” I asked, trying not to act angry.

“You left me when I needed you the most,” she screamed.

“That was your choice, Moncelisa. You asked to be free.”

She shifted in her seat and darted a cold stare in my direction. The tone in her voice when she spoke made me fearful.

"Do you know what I've been going through all these years?" She shoved the gun into my knee, reminding me that she still was in charge.

"Whether I wanted out or not, you should have fought harder for me to stay, we were lovers."

There was no reasoning with this woman. I can say all the things I've done for her since she left us, all the monthly checks she received from TPS, but that would only make her angry. I needed to find a way to get the gun from her. I notice her trying to fight back tears, and my only thought was about my only chance. I waited for her to wipe her eyes, and that's when I pounced. The gun went off, whirling me back across the table, catching me in the chest. This gave her the opportunity to finish what she started.

The room begins spinning. All I could hear were the many people who now realized that we were NOT making a Damn movie. Trying to focus. Trying so hard to focus. Dear God! I saw Moncelisa aiming the gun at my head. I just closed my eyes and waited to see my Jesus.

"Freeze!"

Detectives and police start screaming at Moncelisa, "Drop your gun!"

The paramedics arrived and I ended up in the hospital. Moncelisa was escorted out screaming along the way.

I must've passed out, but maybe I didn't, because when my eyes opened, the room was so bright. She pulled it off! I'm dead. Oh, God! I must be in heaven. I looked to my right and beyond the bright lights to see a room of silver and gold. Beautiful! Then I looked to my left, and there was a shadow forming. It must be one of God's angels. Wow! I am on my way. Death has found me. I could not welcome it. Suddenly, I hear my name being called.

"Curtis." "Who are you? A voice ringed out."

The voice reverberated causing my head to ache. I looked beyond the shadows to a room that was not like the one I envisioned before, but more of a dingy dirt color that, no matter how much you clean it, was just plain dirty. Then I caught a glimpse of Detective Bynum. What is he doing here? Damn! He's in hell also.

"Curtis," the voice said so subtly.

"Come on, man. Open your eyes. Look at me." I open my eyes.

"Man, I am looking at you, and you don't look like Satan! What's going on?" I called on Jesus.

I continue to hear everything going on around me, but I could not talk. I could see my wife crying and weeping but there wasn't a thing I could do. I'm calling out to you! Can't you hear me? There was my beautiful wife. Detective Bynum asked. "Can you hear what I am saying?"

I stayed in the hospital for about a week. My wife by my side. Every time I awake, I asked, "Baby, Who's in charge of TPS?" Just rest Curtis.

She politely stated,"TPS is running on its own. Business is expanding. Curtis, we're going to need a bigger office and a new staff."

"That's your field," I said, my situation wasn't discussed.

She then said, "We're moving in the first week of the month," Once you have recovered.

I laughed and said, "Already done, huh?"

The physical therapy nurse came to take me down to therapy. Lavonia said she'd call later. We kissed and she left.

After therapy, the doctor stated that I can go home and would have a nurse to look in on me from time to time. I called Von to pick me up because I know Lavonia would be busy like always. I waited downstairs for Von to arrive.

Finally, he showed up. Took me by my house to change and dropped me off at the office. The staff greeted me in the lobby, and when Lavonia sits watching, everyone crowds me, and she didn't have a clue.

"Welcome back, Curtis." Once the crowd cleared, there's the queen to this king.

She said, "It's good your home. Why didn't you tell me?"

I stated that I just got the released. We went to my office, and then we talked.

"Let's go to lunch," she said.

So, we left, but not to lunch. She took me to a two-story, eight-room office with a conference room and a little extra.

"You like it, baby?"

"Oh, it's beautiful; in the heart of Atlanta."

It is huge and now its TPS & Associate new location. Now, with the new office, and with the building of the prayer service and Children out of Israel on the move, this gives time to build on God's other projects. Plus putting up the tents and YMA (Youth Ministries Agency) to soon come to the surface. But how can I work on this now with a trial coming up soon? Maybe I just need to focus on this. So, I called a meeting to explain what the future vision holds, expectations, and that I need commitment and loyalty. Also, to appoint a Junior Executive to help Lavonia when she needs help. But who? Going to have to pray on this and allow her to help me make the decision. We have not yet discussed the fatal decision I made before so as you know I'm saying nothing. My brother called me while questioning Desiree and Dre.

"Curtis, did you know that they are twins?"

"No," I said. Do they have any involvement with this deception?

We talked for a moment and then hung up. I'm sitting at my desk just thinking all that God has done for Moncelisa, but she still hated me. The question is still unanswered. Who stole the money? And where did the rest go? Why was it not recovered? Still a mystery. The money was not found.

The trial was about to begin for the murder of my brother. I called my attorney, Wayne to set an appointment to find out what will happen with the twins, what pleas he recommends before the court date. Will there be federal charges, since they were also deceived by Moncelisa until she just told them recently that I am their father. I did not now that I was their father. They had nothing to do with the murder of my brother, but for Moncelisa and Mike there was no hope.

The phone rang. It was my boo. She asked me to come home. Not in a fearful voice but with desperate attitude. So, I left for home. When I arrived, she greeted me with a hug.

“Sit down, Curtis. I want to talk with you about the twins. Do you believe these are your children?”

“Um, you know, Baby with all that’s happened, I have not had the time to really investigate it. All I can tell you is we were in love, at some point in life.

Maybe she wasn’t sure if she was pregnant from me. My mind was racing again. Time to set up for a blood test to seek the truth, not by Moncelisa's word because Desiree and Dre don't look like nothing like my children.

So the medical technician was called to visit the jail for blood samples. "Thank you, Lavoina, for opening my mind," I told her. Then Wayne called with a date to meet with me over dinner a O'Charley's. After dinner, the discussion came about stating that the twins could receive three to five years in prison, and five years probation if they had something to do with it. "Curtis, If you don't press charges, probation with one to three years of community service. I do suggest that you really think about this. Has the blood test returned?" He asked.

"No." I replied.

"Meanwhile, if not are you going to press charges?"

"I am not sure, bro, what to do at this point. All I do know is that I need closure to go on with my life with Lavonia and our unborn. We will have to wait on the blood test to continue this discussion about the twins. I thank you for this moment to discuss the case. I will be in touch."

We went out separate ways. I arrived home, and Lavonia waiting with a smile.

"Curtis, it is time. My contractions are closer."

And at the same time her water broke. I called Lavonia's mother and the Doctor. I grabbed her bags and put them in the car. The only thing, while turning the ignition, I forgot Lavonia! With fear and desperation, I ran back into the house. She was sitting there laughing.

"Slow down, baby. It's going to be okay."

So I took her by the hand headed out the door with her laughing about how I left her. When we arrived, Lavonia's mother and a few close friends were there to greet us.

"Your room is ready, Mrs. Turner. The doctor will be with you within the hour.

I called my mother and told her Lavonia is in labor and I will call on the results.

She said, "I will be praying."

We hung up and I returned to Lavonia's side. Hours passed. No birth. The doctor called me to the side and stated complications with the birth may cause death to either.

Oh, no! Not this! I screamed. I went to the family room to speak with our family and friends. They all went to the chapel to pray to the God of our understanding. For hours, we were in prayer; for twelve hours. Still no birth. I left to be with my wife. They talked about the situation.

Lavonia said, "Curtis, the child needs a life. I have had mine, if by choice, let it live.

"Nonsense! Don't talk like this!" I said with tears in my eyes. "We are going to be okay."

God will see this through. He always does.

Lavonia went into a coma. The alarm sounded from her room. The doctors and nursing staff ran into her room.

"Clear he room."

I couldn't watch what was going on? I went back to he chapel, explained to the family, and prayer became stronger as if the room shook. The everything got quiet. The door of the chapel opened. Its was the doctor.

"Curtis, I 'm sorry. We lost them."

"No! No!" Everyone screams, then a miracle!

"Dr. Long, please return to room 41."

"She's been revived," Her mother said! And the baby was born. They're both in stable condition. It's a beautiful five-pound girl."

Everyone with joy and tears gave thanks to God. I ran to the room where she was sleeping. I couldn't see the baby yet. It was getting cleaned up and tested. I sat by the bed holding my wife's hand as she slept. Then I began to pray and to Thank God for His deliverance. For hours, she slept.

The nurse came by to take me to see our daughter. She's beautiful. A gift from God, who survived the worst.

Everyone's praying for the recovering of Lavonia, and it happens. She awakened, not knowing what had happened.

I explained everything, from death to life. She cried for a while.

"Can I see our baby?"

The nurses brought the child to her. The nurse said,

"This is a miracle child blessed by God. You both fought to be here with a destiny."

The nurse brought the child to her. The nurse said, "This is a miracle child blessed by God. You both fought to be here with a destiny."

Lavonia shouted, "That's it!" Destiny said.

She shouted her name and they smiled at each other. "If this is what you want to name her, then that will be her name."

Destiny! They repeated the new edition name in unison. "Destiny, the miracle child. All the family members greeted and prayed over the child, said their goodbyes, and let us o be with each other. We sat and held each other until all three fell asleep.

A week passed.

The lab called with the results of the blood test for the twins. The test was positive. Not just one child to case about. Now, there was three. I called my attorney to ask the judge to set bond for the twins so that I could visit them. Soon, three days had passed. Lavonia and the child were in good condition, and able to leave the hospital. Lavonia's mother moved.

The lab called with the results of the blood test for the twins. The test was positive. No jus one child to care about. Now, there were three. I called my attorney to ask he judge to set bond for the twins so that I could visit them. Soon, three days had passed. Lavonia and the child were in good condition, and able to leave the hospital. Lavonia's mother moved in to take care of them because, now, I had a lot on my plate.

"Baby, take care of this so tithe we can move on with our lives."

"I will, Lavonia. I will."

I went home to my man cave out back and prayed to God about this sidebar. I hung out in this place of peace for about an hour, and said, "Thank you, Lord." and left.

While leaving to get of my car, my daughters and nine grands showed up from nowhere. It's been a while, so I was surprised. With tears in my eyes, I greeted my family with his and kisses.

“Come to the house to see your little sister.”

They all came in. Lavonia was so suprised. Again, with hugs, kisses, and gifts. I took the grands to the game room, their favorite hangout. Are they visited, I forgot what was on my agenda, and starred off. I wonder if God is trying to tell me something. But what?

They all came in. Lavonia was so surprised. Again, with hugs and kisses and gifts. I took the grands to the game room, their favorite hangout. After they visited, I forgot what was on my agenda, and starred off. I wonder if God is trying to tell me something. But what?

The kids played all kinds of games. I went to sit with my wife and three daughters. I told them to brace themselves for what I'm about to tell them.

“There's two more members to the family. Twins, a boy and a girl,” who I didn’t know were my children.

"What?" Asked with the expression, "Daddy you've been bad," the girls said.

"I'll let Lavonia explain. I have something to take care of, but not to use the names. I asked them all to stay until I returned.

So, I left. On my way, I called the Varsity and ordered food for everyone; more than enough. Then I called my attorney, Wayne, to talk with the judge about a bond for the twins, and to pay the bond, once it was set.

Two hours had passed, and finally, a bond. I asked to talk with the twins first in a conference room to explain the situation.

The twins stated, "So, you are our father?" Mother said that our father was deceased.

"Yes. The blood test that you took proved it." I said.

I explained everything. They apologized with tears in their eyes, not a clue of what they may have become a part of.

“What's going to happen to our mother?” they asked.

“It's up to the courts. She has serious charges conspiring to murder and stealing of funds. I said. I just don't know what's going to happen. We're trying to make a deal with the D.A. We will have to see, but right now, change clothes. I'm taking you home with me until we get some things settled.”

“Can we see our mother?”

“Not today, but in a few days; I'll make it happen. I told them, because visitation is not available at this point.

So, they changed into new clothes, got their property, and headed for home. Wayne talked on the way out the door, and we all went our separate ways.

We arrived at the house, and I asked them to wait on the front deck to talk with Lavonia, because I did tell her I was bringing them home or getting them out on bond. I asked her to meet me at the man cave, and she did. I explained what I had done and that I wanted them to stay here for a few days in one of the extra rooms.

"Curtis."

Lavonia said, "Curtis, my husband, I love you, and whatever you feel you need to do to get this behind us, I'm with your decision."

As always, Lavonia was always supportive of my decisions without misunderstanding.

"Where are they?"

In the front on the deck." I told her.

"Oh!" she said.

"What if I'd said no?"

I smiled.

"I know your heart, baby. You've always allowed God to be in control of me and you followed."

"You know me, huh?"

“Yeah, pretty much. I said. We went to the family room. I said, I'd like for the two of you to meet someone you already know.

I went out to get the twins. “Kids,” Gasping for air while shaking their heads.

Dre and Desiree spoke out, “So, these are our sisters.

“This is your family. They hugged, “This is so overwhelming,” because they, know each other.

I walked off for a moment and asked, “Is this the answer God?” To bring the unknown home to have a family? Or, what?”

“There's extra food, please get something to eat. “Lavonia stated. Baby, you hungry? No, love. I said. She fixed the twins something to eat. I went to the man cave again to thank God.

“Now, I have four daughters and three sons. Seven is a good number.”

I laid down on the sofa in the man cave. No music, No tv, just a peaceful, quiet moment with Jesus. I fell asleep unintentionally, just tired.Hours passed. Lavonia was looking for me. She found me stretched out on the sofa and covered me with a thin sheet and left. The family was still at the house. So, she returned.

“Where's daddy?” Amethyst asked.

"He's asleep. He's been through so much lately.” Wayne called and stated that he's bringing mother, his nieces, and sister to Atlanta this weekend.

“Next weekend, bro, you all come up for the family gathering at the park.”

“You bet!” he said if I’m not called into work in New Orleans.

I thanked Wayne for his support and hung up. The girls said they were going to go to the motel for the night.

“Nonsense!” Lavonia said.

We have plenty of room. Curtis and I will stay in his man cave, if we must. The girls asked, "Are you sure?"

"Of course." I would be pleased to have the family here. There's a knock at the door. Quez and Antwan, had arrived. Now, all the family is here. Everyone is having fun and enjoying each other's company. I was still sleeping, not knowing anything. The evening was long, and Lavonia asked the boys to sleep over in the game room with the grand kids.

With everyone in place, Lavonia went to the man cave and grabbed a few blankets, then crawled onto the sofa with me. She didn't wake me. Just snuggled, prayed and fell asleep. Around seven in the morning, we woke to the aroma of breakfast waiting on the table in the man cave with a large card saying: We love you guys very much. Everyone had signed it.

They prayed for the breakfast and this day, then laid the card down. I said, It was a good thing you asked the girls to sleep over. How did you know? I know you enjoy the grands.

I did not know the boys had arrived. Lavonia laughed, but said nothing. She said nothing at all about the boys being here. We took a shower, got dressed, and went to the house from the back door.

Everyone was eating breakfast. I went into the game room and there was another surprise. Quez was present, Antwan. They were holding little Destiny, tripping about who she looks like. All my children looked much like me, except the twins.

"Dad, I know you get around. Never though that these two could be yours. They all drew close together.

Another day the Turner family is together enjoying each other. The phone rang, and it was my attorney.

"Curtis, the trial starts Wednesday at 9:00am, but the two suspects are pleading guilty, and it will only be an arraignment for sentencing."

"Curtis asked, What about the twins?"

"It's a later date."

"Do what you can, bro. I want them with me for now."

"Okay. As you wish."

Two weeks passed. Mike received twenty to life. Moncelisa, five to ten years, But she can be up for parole in three years. The twins went to visit, but Moncelisa was very sick, and they couldn't visit long. Three more weeks passed, and still, she was sick.

The twins' case came up. Curtis took them to court, and they pleaded not guilty. As my brother stated, the judge asked me for my voice on this subject. So, I spoke up. The said, this will resume later.

The District Attorney accepted the plea, and the case was dismissed due to no insufficient evidence. The twins were free. One week later, the phone rang. It was the hospital, and the news wasn't good. Moncelisa had went into a diabetic coma and passed from complications.

"Oh, no!" I screamed.

"How am I going to tell the twins? They never got the chance to speak to her," since the first visit. But they will be okay the Dr. said.

I called them to the family room.

"Sit down. I have very bad news."

I told them. They were stunned, as anyone would be. Lavonia came into the room. I explained to her. She comforted the twins.

Now, it's just not good, "One thing after another. Now, I felt disturbed as if it was my fault, but it's by choices that put one in situations."

"No! Don't you dare!" my wife said.

The twins called their family and left to meet with them.

In Warner Robins the next day, I stated that I would take care of everything. Three days passed. The funeral came around then everyone grieved in their own way.

They bought a house in Atlanta, Georgia. This was a long, sad year for the family, but by the grace of God, Curtis and the new family will begin to live their new lives.

The end

By Curtis E. Turner

Curtis E. Turner

Bio

Curtis E. Turner is an American resident of Warner Robins, Georgia, Houston County. He currently resides there with his family.

Deceived by Blood

+=======================================

WE ACCEPT SDI®, ETH, USD, AUD, CAD, EURO, NZ CREDIT, DEBIT, DEBT AND EQUITY

LEGAL NOTICE

LEGAL PUBLISHED NOTICE

MOGHUL LIFE STATE, FEDERAL, INTERNATIONAL, UNIVERSAL, WORLD AND KINGDOM COPYRIGHT AGREEMENT

SOI LIFETIME COPYRIGHT PROTECTION®

§104 Unpublished works are also covered under this agreement through-The works specified by sections 102 and 103 while unpublished are unpublished are subject to copyright protection under this title without regard to the nationality or domicile of the author.

Arbitration treaty. Signed, Washington DC, October 22, 1928, entered into force February 12, 1929

All products purchased of the 'brand' are subject to the same laws of Amun et Ih Wachi Nations® Constitution, Laws, Orders and Imperial Charter®, Soi, Republic®, and the Soi Empire®. You are to respect the legal rights of all of our product(s) or we shall go to the extent of pressing charges, filing a legal claim in the Defendants (Court of their Jurisdiction), against those who make claims against our intellectual property. This means that you are to not, sell, endorse, lend, nor infringe on the rights of any copyrights, works, trademarks, patents, photographs, images, videos, or ideas of the said entity without a prior written request or written consent. All rights to this book belong to the sole custody of the controller and the owner of said works "Deceived by Blood," the party who all rights are protected under the Alpha and Omega Constitution®, Amun Privacy Act®, and shall not be violated by anyone wishing to do business with the said entity whether public or private, whether commerce, or non commerce. All rights to the characters from this novel belong to Soi Republic® Intellect Division. All works upon death of the owner and controller shall be left as an inheritance to the estate to the estate beneficiaries. The beneficiaries being the heirs & heiress of this works, Successors.

All products purchased of the 'brand' are protected under private security agreements and are subject to the same laws of Soi Republic Nation®, and the Soi Empire®. You are to respect the intellectual rights, legal rights to our product. This means that you are to not, sell, endorse, nor boot leg, infringe on the rights of any copyrights, works, trademarks, patents, photographs, images, videos, or ideas of the said entity without a prior written request or written consent. All rights to this book belong to the sole custody of the controller and the owner, the party who all rights are protected under the Alpha and Omega Constitution®, Alpha Privacy Act®, and shall not be violated by anyone wishing to do business with the said entity whether public or private, whether commerce, or non commerce. All rights to the characters from this novel belong to Soi Republic®. All works upon death of the owner and controller shall be left as an inheritance to the estate. The beneficiaries being the heirs & heiress of this works.

Terms and Conditions of Use

The literary words and works are not to be reproduced, sold, or traded for money or any reason without written or legal consent. This book was created only for the user intended for whether the purchase was made by the intended user or purchased as a gift for the intended user. The physical copy of this book

"DECEIVED BY BLOOD," purchased itself may NOT Be sold to another party, nor entity.

Returns and Exchanges

Refunds may be made from the store of purchase. Deceived by Blood may not be copied nor reproduced for sales by anyone without written, legal consent. In order to return or exchange, the book must be unmarked with any writings in pen or pencil, this includes autographs. The physical condition must be the same condition in which it was in prior to the day of purchase. There are no exchanges made on books purchased during a book signing.

LIBRARY CATALOGUE

Deceived by Blood has been catalogue at the Soi Library of Justice® as an aboriginal title and at the Library of Congress as a notice to all. All Rights to the DECEIVED BY BLOOD are reserved as aboriginal title.

SOI JURISDICTION®

This books original jurisdiction is under the Soi Republic Nation® first and is not subject of NO OUTSIDE Government nor outside jurisdiction.

SOI LIBRARY OF JUSTICE®

All numbers, works, soi data, intellectual property, digital assets, digital currency, soi dalli ice, soi dalli rich cash, and all assets are held in private trust and may not be used in public nor private without written legal consent from the publisher. This literary works and its components have been insured and bonded in the amount of three million dollars and zero hundred cents Soi Dalli Ice® Cash and Digital Money.

SOI DALLI ICE®, SOI DALLI RICH CASH®

All rights reserved globally to soi dalli ice®, soi dalli rich cash®, Serial Number SD00000009®, ß∂^4-222 Public and Private Tender, One Thousand Dollar Notes (mustard yellow, gold, red, emerald green, gold, black and white) in unlimited amounts, Sealed by the Humes Imperial Medallion [Red, Emerald Green and Gold] as the Official Currency of Soi Republic Nation® and shall be released in multiple notes

Soi Library Catalogue Number® 0309042028

Soi Library Registration Publication Number DECEIV-C-888-0-5 Paperback, ISBN 979-8-9859758-4-0 COPYRIGHT NUMBER TC-77-080-051, SPISBN 66-7-386-66329-51

Digital Data: Soi Digital International Number 0808, TC-77-080-052, 66-7-386-66329-52, DECEIV-C-888-0-5 Deceived by Blood

Assignment has been made on all numbers and private property held in private trust.

REGISTERED BOND NUMBERS

Aboriginal Title Record Delivered, Deposited through the United States Postal Office

LEGAL DISCLAIMER

Fiction Works

Deceived by Blood is a supreme aboriginal title.

Ordering Information:

To order, Quantity sales. Special discounts are available on quantity purchases by book stores, retailers, boutiques, corporations, associations, public relation & advertising agencies, and others. For details, contact the publisher at the address above. Orders, Please contact our partner Moghul Life Publishing Department: moghullife@gmail.com +1 (347) 560-9124

Cover Designed by MONI'SOI **I** IOS'INOM'®

Formatted by moni'soi®
Edited by Shanice Henry
Treaty with the Creeks 1866, Treaty with the Delawares

Patience is Virtue Wait for the Curtis E. Turner Film

Gratitude for Supporting A Moghul Read

Made in the USA
Columbia, SC
04 May 2023